THE BOX SOCIETY

By

G.D. Evans

ISBN: 9781983007330

DEDICATION

Dedicated to Charlie Willmott.

CONTENTS

ACKNOWLEDGMENTS

Many thanks to all my friends who have supported me throughout this process.

PART ONE

663

Chapter One

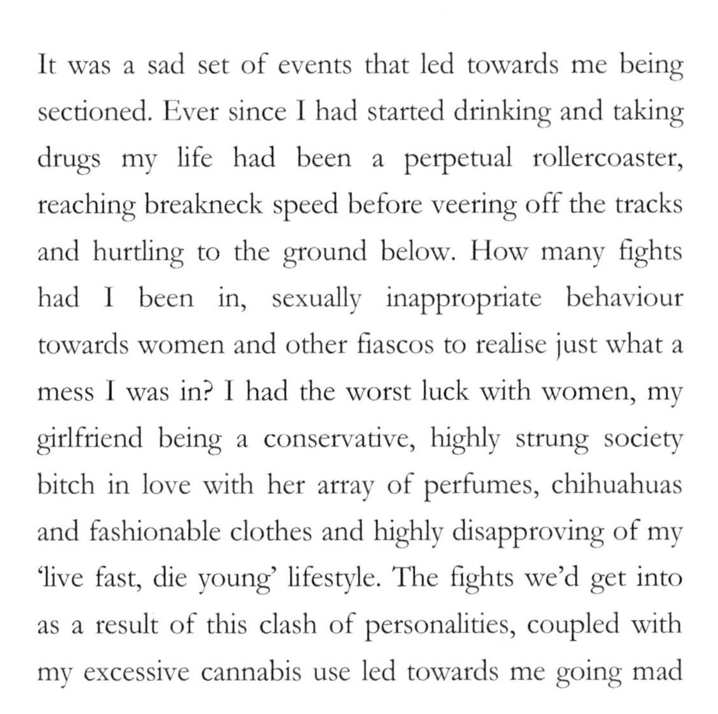

It was a sad set of events that led towards me being sectioned. Ever since I had started drinking and taking drugs my life had been a perpetual rollercoaster, reaching breakneck speed before veering off the tracks and hurtling to the ground below. How many fights had I been in, sexually inappropriate behaviour towards women and other fiascos to realise just what a mess I was in? I had the worst luck with women, my girlfriend being a conservative, highly strung society bitch in love with her array of perfumes, chihuahuas and fashionable clothes and highly disapproving of my 'live fast, die young' lifestyle. The fights we'd get into as a result of this clash of personalities, coupled with my excessive cannabis use led towards me going mad and believing I was a prophet. A prophet whose job it was to warn people that the spirits in my head had prophesied a time that paedophilia would be widely accepted, in the same way it was accepted in ancient Greece. You can imagine what sort of response this got. Within a couple of days, I had lost all my friends and the following week I was homeless, thankfully managing to find a place in a local hostel. However, the psychiatrists soon had a hold of me and I was to find out just what a humiliating, demeaning and life-destroying experience staying in a mental hospital actually is.

Mental health is the only form of healthcare in which the objective is to break the patient down totally to get a docile, obedient slave. They do it through coercion, bullying and drugs. The Aripiprazole pill I was put on made my eyes red and sore, robbed me of sleep and made it impossible to sit down without considerable discomfort. I felt intensely suicidal and despairing. I started off in the ward by answering back whenever the staff were rude and dismissive to me and found this was just a ticket for the staff to keep me there for longer. That isn't healthcare, it's blatant discrimination. The mental health diagnosis makes it acceptable for people to treat you differently from the rest of the population, treating any outburst of anger, sadness or any other negative emotion as if all of it is a symptom of your so-called sickness. They even throw positive emotions into the mix, calling them 'mood elation'. No-one caught in the system is safe from this treatment. In the meantime, they'll go out and see someone getting angry outside of the mental health environment and they can't do anything. Inside of that environment, however, there's no limits to how much they'll depersonalise you and treat you like you're somehow a lesser individual.

I walked up and down the corridors, haunted by visions of me as an old man with a walking stick, going up and down until I collapsed. It's very easy to feel like you'll be inside that system forever once you're in it and my restlessness was an excuse for them to keep me in there for longer. I was getting sick of hearing the same goddamned pop music blasting out of the TV room. There's only so much Justin Timberlake, Rihanna and Sia you can take before those songs start to really grate on your will to live. Months went by and I became accustomed to the discomfort, the occasional cigarette break and the fact that my girlfriend had found new love elsewhere. I was truly a slave, mind, body and soul. I wished for death and then… a bomb went off. I was buried under the rubble and within a few seconds I was dead.

I woke up in a desert after a long rest. I saw what was in front of me and scarcely believed it. It was a series of boxes, eerily standing out from the bleak yet beautiful desert landscape. Six blue boxes were arranged on the left and six red boxes on the right. Each gave out a soft electrical hum, their five sides glowing with a vivid fluorescence. At the end of the rows of boxes was a circular garden with a pure white halo surrounding it.

A man in a white coat emerged from behind the first blue box on the left.

"Hello, I am the doctor, conductor of the 663 experiment," he said. "Here you will learn the true meaning of existence. All the tests and trials of your time on the earth find their fruition here where your soul now awakens. Where you are standing is a world in its own right that receives the souls of dead men and women from your dimension. Each of these boxes contains virtual reality equipment with a specific program for each one designed to stimulate you, give you a fun ride. I'll be monitoring you in the meantime, checking those alpha waves, infiltrating your synapses. I reckon I should tell you where you are and about the inhabitants of this planet. The citizens of planet Albatross are split into two factions, the 666 communities and the 777 communities. The 666 communities have technology built into their bodies and the 777 communities are a bunch of spiritual hippy freaks; 777 inhabitants live in nature while the 666 bunch live in tower blocks."

I noticed a long-haired couple emerge from the garden at the end of the boxes.

"Who are they?" I enquired.

"Oh, they're now part of the 777 community. Somehow, they made it through the red boxes. Funny, that. Oh, by the way, those VR experiences are very real. It may occur to you that it's a strange oddity for Purgatory to be a scientific experiment."

"It didn't occur to me but now that you mention it…"

"All part of God's divine plan, God of course being the ruler of the 777 communities. He also designed all the technology of the 666 communities as well as this box experiment. You worship him on your planet of course, unless you're Richard Dawkins." The couple levitated and flew off into the distance.

I was led to the first box chamber. The doctor opened the door to reveal the man who was inside. The man rushed to me, telling me all of the wonders he had seen in his mind and how my opening the door had released him from the internal machinations that tortured him day by day.

I was then connected to the virtual reality equipment in the box by the doctor and while the things I saw aroused me sexually and emotionally, I could not touch them. They danced around me, images of scantily-clad women merging into one another, their eyes staring wildly. The image penetrated deep into my skull and I saw my hand moving through the women as if they were ghosts. They made high-pitched squeaks and their images convulsed in ecstasy. The background to the scene was pure white, a bright shining light contrasting heavily with the flamboyant colours of the women. The women disappeared and an eye stared at me from the white background.

"Welcome to the blue boxes," said a deep, booming voice. "We are pleased to welcome you here, for life is but an illusion and here you will find illusions to satisfy your mind, body and soul. May God the designer bestow his blessings upon you. Soon it will be time to depart from this first box and continue your trip in the others. These are more than just virtual reality experiences, however. These boxes are alive and contain programs intimately connected to the human psyche. They will cleanse your body and soul, preparing you for the tests and trials of the red boxes which contain visions of hell. Oh, weary traveller, worry not about the tests and trials ahead but give yourself over to the heavenly visions found here." The eye disappeared. I woke up. The doctor removed the helmet and smiled widely.

"You may find it odd that purgatory amounts to a scientific experiment but I'm sure you'll find the first half of this experiment very agreeable indeed. The purpose of it is to cleanse you by showing you the positives of God's creation so that you may be one with him in the Garden of Paradise at the end. You will then be initiated into the 777 communities where you will live in perfect harmony with nature." I was confused.

"How come I need to go through virtual reality in order to get to paradise?" I said. "And why did the voice tell me the visions were real?"

"Your mind is real," said the doctor, "yet its interactions are finite. You will experience all of the beings that exist inside the program, works in progress designed to please the 666 communities. You know of course that 666 is the number of the beast. The mark of all the inhabitants of the 666 communities is that they can now only experience life through technology. This is a test and your successful completion of both the blue and red boxes will determine whether you enter the 777 communities or the 666 communities."

"Only a few moments ago you said it was a certainty that I would get into the 777 communities," I cried in protest. "Now you say the outcome is dependant on how well I perform? Are you trying to trick me?"

"You were a drug addict in the past and it may very well be that you want to escape from these realities," said the doctor. "We will decide what's best for you. Don't try to escape, there's no food or water for hundreds of miles."

That was it then. With reluctance I moved towards the second box.

*

I lived down on an estate in Croydon. My approach to studying was slothful but I had thus far maintained a sleight of hand with regards to social relationships.

I tried to avoid the unpleasant, narcissistic and conformist structure of various clubs which played a large part in an unhealthy love of the social spectacle. The presence of spectacle within culture had long been something that bored me. To me, life was far more about the delicate balance between attributes of living such as consumption of drugs, socialising and sex and keeping at bay certain autistic tendencies from my youth.

I had long lived under the unsettling label of Asperger's which hovered over my head in many social situations. It did not help that I had a nonconformist attitude to culture and dialogue, something my psychiatrist disapproved of.

I smoked pot at this time, a little traditional favourite from my parents' youth that had mutated into this arrogant little adolescent brat called Skunk. He was often by my side enhancing sex, food and other pleasures of the body. Funny how one loses all interest in the demands of culture when consuming a genetically modified herb.

My girlfriend, a young Indian girl of twenty-one who went by the name of Hali often lay next to me on Persian rugs, bong at the ready for the devotional prayers to Shiva. We often talked about love and in increasingly sentimental tones just lay there, bonded by foolishness. It was supposed to be the twenty-first century but I often felt that I was stuck in a different time zone. I listened to Hali's sweet, poetic and songful voice.

One day, Hali became a Christian. Didn't last very long but she's quite indecisive. For a moment I was dumbstruck. I'd always pictured Jesus as a perverse and extreme sadomasochistic freak. It was hard, however, not to be turned on by her sweet voice singing seductively: "I love Jesus and I pray that all the saints and apostles come and bless this holy sanctuary."

She turned on Beethoven's Symphony No. 7 to prove her point.

"Look," she said in a nauseatingly sincere voice. "It is God's gift of music."

I didn't know what to say.

"I feel a little cross about this," I said.

"Well you're hung quite well, aren't you?" she replied in jest. I still hadn't won this futile battle.

"Look, of all the things you'd want to be, why a Christian? You going down to one of those awful happy-clappy congregations? It's unheard of in my family."

"Interesting. I heard someone tell me that he had the clap."

"Ah, must have been a poet!"

She looked at me and smiled sadly.

"It is beautiful what you poets do. You educate us about our bodies. But then you need so much cultural junk in order to be as poetic in the workplace as you are in bed! It's what other people think of you that depresses you poets.

"I remember a little girl; her name was Rachel. Her body was covered in leprous sores. She sought sanctuary in a community of S&M people. Their most derided and hated character was a man called Fantasy. They hated Fantasy because he was a chronic masturbator who never tidied his room. The man was deeply spiritual however, yet he was a thief. Thieves drive bargain economies because to them everything is a bargain. They never see the value of anything but they cry when they're good thieves. They then become cowards and the cowards try to prove that they're strong by not getting the number 666 tattooed on their foreheads.

"You see, they want to see this happen in the outside world but they also don't want to see the outside world. Thieves are submitted to culture by intelligence. They often come from deluded families with family members who practice spiritual rituals at Holy Spirit churches where they worship under the illusion that they can ignore Solomon's wisdom. These are often families that try to live like Revival communities from Canada. Canadians practice rites that can most accurately be dated to the time the Roman Empire drove the false economy of Caesar into the ground by finding God through the sinner's path when everyone was trying to live the holy way.

"Only the best and the brightest amongst them would have had that ability and they would have been able to induce seizures in lepers by healing their sores through the blood of Christ and not Jesus. Jesus was a man who considered his path to be the Son of Man as he would have been the representative child of the holy communion in the Garden of Peace; the Snake interfering through temptation. They were living in holy submission to their holy father by not touching him and their bond to him was broken through mishap. The mistake of slave culture was heard by Kings and Queens who practiced witchcraft.

"Their magick was a classic mistake of getting what they wanted the easy way. There was no pollution in the air until a sandstorm approached. The deep evil of the two lonely ascetics, Adam and Eve, was considered an insult to the Holy Virgins who practiced their painless art of chastity to best effect through castration. Their illnesses were the fault of a man who felt pleasure rather than pain. The Father stood above their baths and mocked them for their holy pride before testing their chastity amongst rapists. The most disliked man (an overgrown infant) was put in the body of a Pharaoh King who was subjected to animalistic environments that were fucked up by interstellar time travellers throwing their most amusing false economies into other time zones.

"False notions of architecture prevailed in the twentieth century and consumers of music were then given a cultural trash junkie debt monger called MJ, placed amongst children to tell them why he preferred cool to hot. He was a grown man's idea of The Fool on the Tarot deck and thought it was a good idea to mimic healing ceremonies associated with rebirth in a culture that does not understand life.

"He was talking about the human race and his arrogant hatred of the intelligentsia; excommunicated Masonic families caused cultural chaos when certain healed schizophrenic mindsets thought that their minds controlled other minds. These men and women, when healed, are forced to practice spiritual techniques as a result of drug addiction which fuels false emotions and negative attitudes to life.

"In such bodies, miracles occur and they see the spiritual path as wise. Their wisdom is not revealed to anyone in the know. Not when they are forced to see value in things they don't understand. That's the problem.

"People want to feel AIDS in solemn silence and not by the worthless teenage trash left over in an overgrown man living in a mental health block. It is the way of adults to bully and malign failures and to give them tests to prove their virtue. They cannot practice indifference because temperance failed. After the initial head-rush of Jesus, they become obsessed with conspiracies and fantasies of ghosts and werewolves. Their minds are driven by pseudoscience as opposed to science and fear lurks in their minds because of the genetic memory of how abracadabra, one, two, three, never worked out.

"They hate tattoos, pain and the number 666 which implies body art. Body art is a symbol of the failure of an artist to become an artist and it used to be practiced through fear, brainwashing and torture by the most non-consensual amongst us. The cultural, rippling patterns of paranoia spark fears in comedy writers and western culture retaliated by punishing poets.

"It is the most serious writers who suffer in a media-obsessed culture because they do not synchronise well with other people due to the infantile notion amongst mad scientists that Jung is not for poets.

"A culture that can no longer accept pain, suffering and guilt creates worse pain through imposing suffering on autistic, schizophrenic, bipolar, Asperger's syndrome, depressive and personality disorder types because they talk the way I do. My ways are over and British culture will be taken over by an Indo-Aryan tribe member. You!"

"My dear Hali, I am a laughing stock already in your eyes!

"You know, Kafka is one of my favourite poets. But his poetry is the slingshot of negativity, a twisted facsimile of the stone that hit Goliath. His poetry is of a man who didn't sin who faces punishment for ignoring the final sin that didn't make it. Ignorance is bliss and is only accepted by the purest amongst us and cultural leftovers from pre-Raphaelite eras where primitives had no notion of death.

"Life Magick is Death Magick in the eyes of stupid men and women who want to preserve their relatives and make Hippocratic oaths to the Son as opposed to the father. Jesus was an S&M psycho! I've told you so many times! I dream about his laughing on the cross! Hurling abuse back at the crowd who are now bathing in his blood! Are you perhaps recognising now why they killed artists in the Dark Ages as opposed to witches? It's one of the known cheats in the book to live the life that Kafka lived and it happens to only the most perverse amongst us. People lose kindness by seeing the beauty in evil. Even jewellery and body piercings count in certain communities, you know. And those communities protect the innocence of evil by adding impurities to the filth projected through chronic masturbation and addictive behaviour as opposed to ghetto-compulsive hustling manifestations of this crap.

"You see the addiction of Machiavelli? People hate TRUTH that much! As far as I'm concerned, Truth was Number One. But only special people are Number One and culture gave the folly of the great geniuses to the spoiled children of America through the psycho-fantasies of British youth. Fantasies dreamt by the intelligent fools of the… Politics? I do not like that idea. The bureaucratic notion of intelligence being put to the test by idiots with big books does my nerve endings in!"

"Too much weed tonight, dear! I'm going to enjoy a little more than you tonight, you kinky fantasy fetish! Ah, like a little doormat that I can walk over!"

Chapter Two

The doctor led me to the second box and attached me to the VR gear. I shifted to a higher plane of consciousness for a few seconds. A blind man walked to a fountain surrounded by his lovely trio of angels.

"Where are you taking me, divine travellers of the night?"

"We are here beside you, we have always been here for you, even when the Son of Man healed you, and we guided you from the ritual of sores to the Fountain of Life."

The fountain was built of decayed marble stone; a faded mosaic constituted the outer structure and the angels poured water over the man's face.

Flames burst through his eyes and he screamed in agony and ecstasy, "I am burning with fire!"

I transferred myself to a local field where there

were sheep, obeying instructions from a black sheep. They approached me with grass in their mouths and when I opened my hand to them they dropped grass in it. From across the field, the black sheep said sheepishly, "Eat it! It is good for you." I obeyed and was rather surprised at the unique sweetness of the taste. When the sheep was satisfied that I had enjoyed it he said that it was a special privilege that the flock had prepared and in unison, the sheep bowed their heads in respect. They then moved around in circles, triangles and squares saying their own names. I heard an alien voice say the word 'identity'. Then the sheep magically disappeared and in their place was left the symbol of Solomon's seal.

I looked and surveyed the landscape. I saw three hills and on those three hills I saw three crosses and a distant voice said, "I hope we have the measurements right."

A silhouetted figure walked away from the cross on the left. I walked towards it, making my way through flowery meadows, enjoying a mellow variety of sensations. The smell seemed so pure and healthy and even mud seemed to have a life-giving quality about it. As I moved closer to the hill something extraordinary happened and a white, serpent-shaped fire moved up the cross and turned into a bright shining white light at the top. From that white light an image manifested itself and a human body of pure light emerged and consumed the cross itself. The body glowed and the fire went inwards as a man with stars shining in his body emerged. A ring of fire appeared before him and the star body leapt through the ring and both the body and the ring vanished into thin air. Then two more portals opened up in front of the right and left crosses and two men emerged from behind the crosses. One threw some guns through a portal and said, "There you go," and the second threw some sticks of dynamite through the other portal and said, "There you go."

I ran up the second hill and looked through the portal. Through it were four people standing in a room looking perplexed at the guns laid out in front of them. The second one, I was looking into a hospital room and the man there had a manic look in his eye. I tried to enter but a voice yelled, "Stop! It is not permitted for you to enter!" I looked around for the source of the voice, finding nothing. When I turned back the portals had disappeared.

I walked down the other side of the hill and noticed a lake, glittering pure blue in the sun. There were some swans swimming in the lake in formation, running ripples through the water that sparkled joyously. The sun shone warmly over this scene and I started to feel sleepy. I lay down in the grass and dropped off.

A dream within a dream. An angel came to me and sung a song in a melody that was so entrancing, I broke down in tears at its haunting quality, thanking God for sending me this moment.

It sang:

"Life is but a dream in the boxes of paradise.

The illusions of the fabric of time,

Let God guide your soul beyond illusion to the truth

And bless your soul with eternal youth."

I woke up, first by the lake and then again for real in the box. The doctor removed my headgear and led me outside. "Do you remember why you were put in hospital?" he said softly.

"I think so. I was an addict and I suffered from psychosis as a result," I replied.

"Tell me, how did you find the treatment there?"

"To be honest, it was horrible. They bullied me, humiliated me and the nurses violently attacked some of the patients, especially the ones who refused to take their medication. What was worse was that many of the nurses professed a faith in Christ. One of them even told me he was blessed to go to heaven minutes after he'd brutally medicated an uncooperative patient. They're blind, totally blind. Here we have a brutal machine designed to break you down, no real displays of love or forgiveness there. At one point I lost it completely with them, protesting hopelessly and manically at their torture. But it was no use. You are seen as a lesser individual. The people running the system cater to this public stereotype. I personally believe I was under a curse. The thing about hell that most intrigues me is that there are dimensions to it. A whole structure designed to imprison those caught hearing voices and being delusional. And now that I see things through virtual reality I somehow feel more alive. Yet somehow I fear what I'll see in hell. I can't help but feel that I predicted seeing these images. Yet I still can't figure out, why in death? All my tests, trials and tribulations on Earth amounted to this? Virtual reality boxes?"

The doctor smiled a broad grin. "Souls are energies floating around in the ether having left their previous bodies. We have the science to create replica bodies of souls we select. We have a complete breakdown of your memory system and how it operates. Your complete past life was analysed thoroughly before we revived you in this body. This is a premature birth. Your soul is still endowed with some of its past-life memories. You shall be cleansed of all earthly attachments. I should mention that we are somewhat sympathetic to your cause on Earth. Drugs at least started with the usual goals of expanding one's mind and reaching heights of pleasure. But then you shouldn't have *snorted* drugs, should you? Not if you valued your nose. Your nose is restored now, however. We don't snort drugs on this planet. But the mushroom provides all the 777 communities with mind expansion. Once a soul is found here it is provided with either the 666 programming or the 777 programming by ETERNALBOTCo. Yes, a project designed to provide all travellers with either eternal paradise or eternal dream. Us scientists knew we'd found a home for all sorts of souls.

"We refer to the 666 prisoners as virtual autistics. They have no choice but to obsess over whatever subjects are beamed into their technology via wi-fi. Here we have a whole internet communication underground, a machine that lives and feeds on their brains. They live in computer game internal environments, technology far more advanced than the comparatively crude technology in the boxes. It's a topsy-turvy world here, it really is. An experiment with death, time and perception... I guess the reason we have virtual reality here is the sheer wonder of what was built when we added it to the mix. Technology that communicated directly to the brain, creating a dialogue between man and machine... The machine is alive. It thinks. It's real. The reactivation of your past-life dreams is an essential part of this purgatorial experiment. Content from psychosis is also included. Psychosis was a misunderstood condition on your planet. Just because someone gives out negativity doesn't mean you feed them negativity. Yet that is just what countless doctors and nurses did all over the world. And the man who invented the lobotomy won the Nobel Prize. No psychiatrist would enter the 777 communities were he to be found here; 666 is the only way such primitive life can be made to overcome the lies they fed themselves and the patients. For punishing people for illusions and applying powerful chemicals to the brain, they only get to experience illusion, not knowing the difference between the VR dreams and the real world. Your fate may be different. After all, Jesus said, 'Blessed are ye poor!'"

*

"What a world we live in!" said Hali. "Brutal gatecrashers broke into a party me and my friend were in once and took me upstairs to physically punish me. I needed to be punished, you see, being the naughty girl that I am. Even under the innocent gin and tonic exterior, nicely drunk from wine, spirits and beer, I needed that porn film scenario to occur at my party in front of the guests. They chained me to a table and molested me, fondling my breasts and mocking me for my Lord Shiva. It was then that I gave my life to Jesus, free to enjoy my satanic sin even as the blood of Jesus washed me clean. My mouth ached from all the fellatio but I was at their command. There were some bored guests saying they'd much rather watch Breaking Bad, so I told them to change the channel. They pointed the TV remote at us but the image didn't change. As the whipping got more ferocious, some of the good thieves started to cry. They all came in my vagina but I was on the pill so no foetus developed. And now I have Jesus' blood at my command, I grasp the Holy Spirit to feed me heights of sexual ecstasy. How I came to this gnosis is a fascinating one. It started when I was greedily slurping on Marvin's cock. I imagined demons molesting me in hell, self-harming with delight. I realised that all it took was the blood of

Jesus to wash me clean. After all, no-one got punished like Jesus. But as I moved to Gerald's penis the image changed and I heard a voice cry out, 'From the side of Satan comes the blood of saints and from the side of Christ comes the living waters of he who reigns forever and ever.' I saw Satan and Jesus lying dead. Satan was laid on a bed of wicker and Jesus on a marble slab. An alchemical potion was applied to Jesus' mouth and he was revived. Satan was put in a box and whisked away to another planet. 'Such is the fate of those who interfere with God's plan,' said the High Priest, clothed in a red robe. Bibles were burnt to sacrifice words for new life. It was at this point they'd got me in double penetration. 'I give my life to Jesus!' I cried out and the guy doing me in my arsehole cried out, 'No, you give your ass to me first, bitch!" The fucking was intense and every crevice ached afterwards.

"Still, how are you?"

"How am I?" I said. "OK, I guess. My day was filled with shimmers and shadows emerging from some time past when a mental patient entered my life. He said he was the reincarnated soul of a patient who died of a lobotomy. It was now his destiny to be searching for the missing piece of his brain for all eternity. He said that he was the eternal victim, destined to never find happiness. A victim of an earlier age of psychiatry… 'The left and right hemispheres never work in symmetry,' he said. 'I am always getting lost. The bits of my brain that are left are part of plant life. No God is going to intervene here. By destroying my brain, they destroyed my soul. Now I have no home that can rest me, no activities that can satisfy me and no drug that can cure me. They punished me for a thought crime, you see. All of politics was rooted against the nonconformist. I thought I was Jesus, dying on the cross, unable to bear the material bonds I was imprisoned in. I, the original mind imprisoned in matter, flesh that was ripped from my body by the whip. There I saw through the illusion of hell, realising that the lying spirits had better things to do than eternally punishing mere mortals. I saw through Satan's power at that moment, seeing it as an eternal consequence of falsehood but with truth ever in reach. Was there ever such an illusion? The great God in the sky never intervenes but he does punish in the end. The great eternal mind has absolute control over you. There is a mind that knows everything that has happened, is happening and will happen to you. You are at the mercy of this higher power's original intentions. Whatever he planned will come to fruition. The computer game that God plays condemns innocent souls to eternal hell. The only hope is that God changes every negative to a positive. But God won't give me my brain back. And worst of all, God knows there is no necessity for suffering. Yet he commands it. It is an essential part of his design. In order to build paradise, you build hell. One goes up, the other goes down. All of God's most negative thoughts incarnated into pure souls all over the world. Some destined for eternal suffering. All because of his divine plan…'

"I could not see inside him because his soul had become hollow, an empty space overcome with negative energies. God suffers as he experiences paradise. No positive can exist without a negative. If anything is possible then eternal damnation is possible. The blood on the surgeon's hands is not coming off anytime soon. But the surgeon doesn't have to worry because he's not split in two. But now the war is between heaven and hell and who pays the ultimate consequences. For ignoring the prophets of old, the rulers paid the foolish price and gave into Satan's schemes. They build their paradise at the expense of others. At the moment the mentally ill are being punished. Next it could be political dissidents or nonconformists in general. They are destroying all the prophets. The ones who see God are then hounded by merciless demons. But when you're split in two that's where no-one can reach you. Oh, woe for the restless lobotomy victim. Where shall he find a science to rebuild his brain? What lies ahead for him in the future apart from misery and death? Only God knows and only God heals. The force of God vibrates throughout all his creation. That is enough for certain."

*

What a schizophrenic couple me and Hali are! That's how the doctors defined us but we would never want our speech to fit inside a box. Our speech tangented into exquisite musical abstraction as we found new meaning where none previously existed. As the voices hit us we started to telepathically communicate and alchemical symbols flashed before both our eyes. Oh, to lose oneself in the ever-elusive other! Knowing that we would be dead one day, oh what a reason to make love now! I leapt upon her, ripping off her sari and fondling her supple breasts.

"Oh, the wonder of you! I thank the lord for this day, I really do! I feel as if several orbs of pure transcendence were surrounding me right now, beaming love into my alpha waves! Oh, that the doctors at the Bethlem could touch the freedom I feel as I am free to be me with you, our madness creating a gorgeous symphony! Beethoven's 9th has nothing on this vision of freedom. To lose myself in your loving arms while I encircle you as a Black Widow spider destroys her lover! May the holy trinity sanctify our love, our hearts merged together as one!"

Lovemaking between me and Hali works on many different levels, with Hali screaming "James Joyce!" into my pineal gland using her psychic abilities. I flashed whole sections of *Ulysses* as I worked my way up to orgasm. I came long and hard, lines of text from Burroughs and Joyce penetrating my vision.

Chapter Three

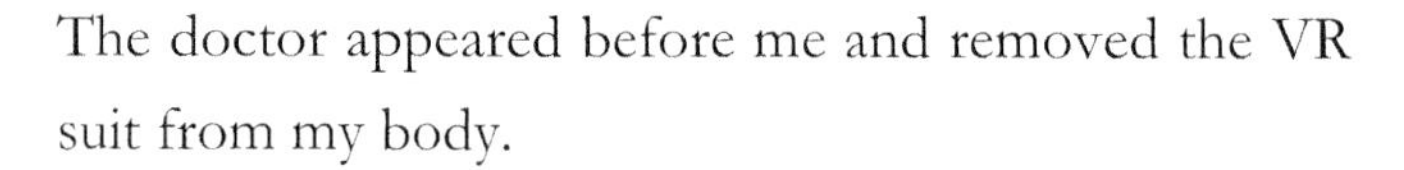

The doctor appeared before me and removed the VR suit from my body.

"There is something you need to understand about what's happened to you," he said, a sympathetic look on his face. "There were a whole team of us at one point. But it didn't work out. In fact, none of the advances in science worked out in the end. In fact, so many economies were driven out of this planet as a result of the pure brutality of this experiment in its heyday that the only choice people had was to go back to nature and sacrifice animals again. When entire populations hear that they have sinned, they naturally blame their mistakes on some pure creature. A man previously considered schizophrenic was suddenly considered to be the greatest prophet who ever lived because he saw in a vision the way scientists drew their positive electrical energy from a pure negative source. The man's religious doctrine acknowledged the existence of a being unknown to us at the time but was later acknowledged as actually being real. We all had to acknowledge the existence of the supernatural at that point and even the uncorrupted doctors were given identity changes so they could join the global movement that led back to organic life.

"The being in question is the most frightening moral paradox and it is the eternal victim. He actually exists. He is an essential part of creation that from the far past to the present and on into the future, has, does and will always suffer. Every time he is incarnated in human form he is tortured inexorably and all the forces of the universe prevent him from having a glimmer of happiness in his life. He is pain incarnate, pure negative electrical energy. Societies that find him use him as a power generator, converting his negative energy into positive energy. He lies under tight clamps, wires penetrating every orifice, and it is considered a great honour by the intelligentsia of any given planet to torture him by draining him of his energy. The public realised that saving him would destroy the whole of life as life is reliant on pain and he is the spirit that creates pain, without which one cannot survive. They decided that the only possible solution to the sheer horror of the fact that anyone coming near him would automatically be drawn to torture him in a pattern of behaviour which became addictive, would be to allow this eternal manifestation of sheer negativity to become a source of electrical power on another planet. The consequences of this on the business of scientific experimentation became obvious to them as the details of scientific experiments were revealed to the public. They could not even begin to grasp that the blood of dead schizophrenics, addicts and alcoholics who had been tortured to death were being used to add emotions to pills, serums and other varieties of drugs and medications.

"One genuine eternal victim existing created the need for doctors and scientists to seize many more victims and drain their life essence from their blood and flesh to chemically create new medications with certain chemical reactions preserved within the makeup of the drug. In other words blood, sweat and tears went into the medications, earning the nickname 'meat' by the more cynical consumers. The unnervingly violent backlash against doctors by certain members of the general public became confused and men of good character were killed alongside the bad ones. Bestial behaviours were now commonplace and many people suddenly disappeared. A huge amount of creatures thought to be extinct seemed to suddenly reappear on the planet and the survival instinct took over. Rescue missions from alien species arrived and any survivors from the scientific, spiritual and political communities were sent to live on other planets. These boxes are the only ones that were kept from many similar experiments. Society mellowed out and human beings are now closer to nature than ever before. Some a little too much so…

"Now I want to show you the boxes. On the left we have the blue boxes and on the right we have the red ones. The blue boxes are the manifestation of the Christ power within man and the right ones are the serpent power that makes its way to the base of the spine. In other words, the blue boxes are paradise and the red boxes are a fiery inferno in which the only comfort is to be had in shadows and reflections. Spiritual transcendence defines the VR blue and chaos is the VR dreams of the red. Beyond these boxes is a circular garden. A garden of paradise. If you saw the boxes from a bird's-eye view you would see that the boxes and the garden form a lower case 'I'. Arial font, I'd say, but hey! I'm old-fashioned. Only really extreme manifestations of behaviour are enough for us to actually have to arrest members of the tribes on this planet but this is the safest way to construct purgatory for anyone. Everyone acts naturally now and the cruel tricks of scientists have left the earth and believe it or not, this is the last mental hospital and the last prison that is permitted to exist on the whole planet. Not to mention that it runs on electricity. Nothing else does here, apart from the bodies of the 666 communities. Any interference with the 777 communities is dealt with swiftly by a magician waving a magic wand and making uninvited visitors disappear. That's how simple it is for them now. Thanks to us opening portals, transporting the unwanted person or object to another location in electrical response to the movement of the wand, the silly hippies think they have magic powers!"

That said, I entered the third box, put on the bodysuit and was now standing outside a house. It was a beautiful cottage in fact; a serene and humble little abode with a familiar and comforting demeanour. Tolkien would probably describe this little haven of security as something akin to the luxurious abode of Tom Bombadil.

There was a gigantic door knocker shaped like a phallus and above it a sign saying: NOT OSIRIS.

I knocked on the door and heard a squelching sound. It went on for a long time, sometimes occurring at regular intervals, sometimes in syncopated time as if the sound had been constructed by John Coltrane himself.

The squelching sound stopped. A voice from within the house. "We have a visitor…"

A woman answered the door. It would be more appropriate to say that WOMAN answered the door. She was an Indian woman of purity and beauty, straight black hair falling right down to her posterior. She had an hourglass figure and a body that seemed to radiate light from within its pure essence. Her face was round, her lips full and her wide eyes had a mischievous quality, luring you in to her inner world.

"I am Hali," she said softly. "My boyfriend and I are a couple and with you we make up a threesome."

She beckoned me in. It occurred to me at this time that the experience felt like a dream. A very beautiful dream where my desires were met perfectly. At the base of her spine was a glorious tattoo, a spider's web. She led me into the living room, bedecked with carpets decorated with pure geometry that is beyond my ability to describe. You see, I could not stop focusing on HER. She was beauty to behold. She turned round to me, her eyes burning with desire. On the ground her boyfriend laid a chiselled, healthy specimen of a man whose penis was very large and stuck up in the air, ready for action.

She smiled warmly. "You know, I love the penis," she said. "Such an innocent thing, yet capable of giving me such sensation, such joy in living. Me and my boyfriend invite you warmly to make love to both of us." As she said this, she sultrily stepped towards me, took my hand and held it against her left breast. "Your penis is small," she said. "Couldn't possibly satisfy those back areas but… I wonder!" She held her hand over my genitals and as if by magic they grew bigger! "Now you can satisfy me!" she said greedily, looking at my bulging stallion. "So hard to choose!" she said, her pupils dilating at the prospect of two genitals instead of one.

I woke up; the doctor removed the bodysuit and the VR equipment. "Your first trip to paradise, eh?" he said.

*

I went to sleep and a few seconds before, Hali's body seemed to shapeshift and became the bodies of various different women. Then a deep blackness overwhelmed me and I started to dream.

Before me were three men and their bodies were filled with stars. I was in the stockroom of a supermarket and there was a hole in the wall that looked out into the galaxy. "You did not join us," they said, and I saw their previous human forms manifest themselves in the bodies and as they faded away they told me that it would be my eternal punishment to throw cereal boxes into the hole in the wall. I picked up the boxes and threw them into the galaxy. As I was pondering the meaning of this I picked up a packet of Ricicles and the sudden realisation of how to leave this prison became obvious to me. I looked behind me to try and find a spacesuit and woke up with a start.

It's always frustrating to be woken up during a meaningful dream and Hali was there with a big beaming smile on her face.

"Let's go shopping!" she said.

"I fancy some cornflakes."

Nothing soothes the soul like a trip to Sainsbury's. After the strange trancelike speech that me and Hali engaged in the night before, the crude colloquialisms of the sarf-east Londoners had a melody all of its own. The marriage of several different voices filling the store had a dissonant quality, like listening to the music of Webern for free. I had taken enough drugs with Hali that all life seemed like music to me.

While perusing the vegetable department, I overheard an unusual conversation, quite unlike anything I'd heard near the Maris Piper potatoes before.

A guy with short, brown, curly hair was talking to an excited-looking ginger-haired guy with glasses who looked like the lovechild of Alan Bennett and Urkel, however unlikely that may sound. The brown-haired guy looked scared and not because he was talking to Alan Urkel. "Look," he said. "I'm quite scared," he said. "Somehow I feel more comfortable near organic potatoes. I had applied to be a member of a secret society because I had a telepathic experience on acid. At a witchcraft ceremony… Heavy! Anyways, they sent me some books and a manifesto. One book was about a woman raped by alien alchemists, another was about a woman who dates an opera singer who believes in fairies and then he rapes her, another was about a philosopher who believes in fairies and also runs a dating service for rapists and the other one was about how we're all getting raped by science! Last night I found a note on my table and it says:

"'Drown yourself, hang yourself, shoot yourself. And then watch movies and films that play these life stories out. Understand the way you relate to yourself and others and then you will be free. Misunderstanding such a path leads to calamity. Feel the shame and sorrow of those who have been neglected and understand that their suffering is due to their wrongdoings. Forgive like Jesus and then send them on Satan's path to allow them to feel pride again. Be sedentary, be promiscuous and remember that to every season there is a time to live, a time to kill and a time to die. Gain knowledge of conservative and liberal politics and enjoy the comforts afforded by their natural social baby communism. Allow communism to mature and flourish and you will see your fear was caused by worshipping your shadow. Do not allow your fear of heights, weight, potential damage or the sex/violence equation to allow you to unwittingly damage yourself. Study philosophy, science, alchemy, drugs, meditation, mediation, revelation, serial murders, autistic individuals, bipolar individuals, sociopathic individuals, psychopathic individuals, schizophrenic individuals… understand your sickness. Understand ancient history, civilisation and culture. Understand your relation to the legal system and see the powerful legal symbols intended to make you fear it. Laugh at how easy it is to avoid getting arrested and understand your decision not to kill, murder, rape and terrorise is only judged by your capacity to indulge in these dark passions of the soul without getting caught by us. We arrest you, we expect you to stay in prison for fear of your presence being known about the world. We have operated under many guises but we are the Illuminati. We don't exist but if we did we would operate underneath an organisation that serves our purposes. When we arrest you, we torture you and treat you like dogs because quite frankly you deserve it. If you want suffering we serve it out on a plate. All we ask of you is to obey and you will find that we are perfectly willing to reward you and we even offer cleansing of the body and soul. See the prison that is your own society, your own mind and your own body and soul and you will gain understanding on how to exist inside a prison. But no-one can set you free except yourself… or U.G. Krishnamurti.'"

"Who's that?" asked Alan Urkel.

"An Indian philosopher…"

I made a mental note to ask Hali about him once she'd chosen between Sainsbury's brand and Kellogg's.

I forgot.

Pity…

Chapter Four

Me and the doctor sat down, resting by the side of the third box on the left, looking out into the desert, and I noticed a motionless robot, about 6' 5" tall, holding a machine gun. There were two lights on his sculpted arse, flashing neon blue and traffic-light red, giving a strange sense of foolishness to his overall demeanour. I say he, he had a male face but decidedly female tits, enclosed within a mechanical bra. In my pre-schizophrenia days on Earth, I'd have associated that sort of thing with some futuristic gay club playing deep house. Now it looked like artificial intelligence and even flinched a bit as it stared out into the setting sun which filled the vast desert horizon with an ambient orange hue.

"Let's smoke a spliff," the doctor said.

"A spliff?" I said, totally alarmed at the prospect of smoking a spliff with a doctor.

"Yes, a spliff."

So we sat down and smoked a spliff. It was good shit, man! Oh boy, was it good, like it was God's own brand or something along those lines. I hadn't enjoyed a spliff this much since 2003. And the sun was going down, with no police officers about except the androgynous robot. I saw two figures on the horizon. Then I saw them lie down together.

"Oh God, I have got to see this!" said the doctor, and he pulled an electrical device out of his pocket and gave it to me. I saw the two figures magnified and they were fucking alright. Doggy, missionary, the works!

"Feel free to have a wank," said the doctor, but I politely declined. Even in death I retained something of the bourgeois upbringing that drove me crazy in life. Not to mention that I'm not gay. I'm really not, you know. Yes, I might be nice, I might be gentle and I might be a good friend to women, a shoulder to cry on and all that, but I'm not fucking gay! That's a fucking stereotype, goddammit!

Anyways, the guy came all over her face and pissed off over the horizon.

Hmm... I thought. *What a peculiar sight to see out in the desert!*

"The man came over her face because men rule

women again," the doctor said, a melancholy expression on his face. In fact, that was the expression that broke him.

"I'm sorry," he said. "That was a lie. There are no words to describe what happened. You used to watch that sort of thing over the internet."

"What do you mean?" I asked politely.

"Well, your day was spent putting drugs up your nose and jacking off to porn. So, no wonder you didn't get laid. When people said 'nice guys finish last', you didn't get it. You were the eternal victim at school. Crying your eyes out, bullied for your autism, intelligence and ego. Battles about truth and knowledge all seem futile now. When you were older you became Dionysian, a perfect version of yourself existed at one point and then it didn't. Remember?"

The doctor explained, "Certain microchips and electronic devices were wired into sleepers' heads and television boxes were removed, as was any manifestation of typical household technology. All holy communities were given potent psychedelic drugs and day and night blurred in their minds, their eyes as a black cat or a red rhubarb. As such, mystical states of consciousness revolved around the 777 communities, which purified through the protective sacraments of the church and the magickal protection of occultic symbols, gained us scientists the perfect opportunity for an observational experiment with certain non-conformal types. They lived in gardens of paradise, special controlled forces of nature which never received any rain until they awoke at dawn and lay down on the grass to sleep at sunset. Violence, anger and other expressions of man's lower behaviours were not even present and the conformal bodies circulated round the non-conformal types. Dancing, everyone was God. The music they listened to was nature's own harmony and melody, the interactions between the ghosts of the air, the birds of paradise and the creatures of the earth. Unlike the 666 communities their bodies did not contain a technological mind.

"In the 666 world, man's greed for electrical technology had befuddled the law who now no longer saw the physical humans as a problem but the very existence of identity itself. Whatever Windows or Apple program emerged lost its user interface and so the law could not tell whether the minds inside the computerised bodies were interacting with real people or with hallucinatory images. In reality, they could no longer feel their bodies but had each become completely internalised, aware only of their programmed life. In other words they were not aware of any sensation in their bodies, their internal reality relating only to the computer program built inside them. The only way for their physical bodies to be active and not decay was an automatic program designed to keep their bodies active. Certain command prompts were built in so that people would walk down the street for their exercise six times a day and occasionally just for laughs, 666 times. Sometimes malfunctions occurred. Such malfunctions made for unique experiences through the telepathic network that connected the minds together at synchronised intervals. The great game-player worked alongside the puppet-master and hidden masters to control the masses from invisible astral ships. Games involving the manipulation of their bodies were watched from above as a submissive population were jerked around by Control's game. It was hilarious to observe this as people contorted into ever more amusing positions. Losing pain and all external feeling from their bodies was part of the way certain 777 individuals were given free reign to pull anyone's scrotum skin halfway down Wall Street. The silly hippies had heard that the scrotum skin was stretchy and flexible enough to be stretched round the world twice. Those were the days! The amusement of some outcasts from the 777 communities was enough, for now people bound by the beast of matter were playthings for them. The holy ones fought real-life battles during their tenure, most enjoying the obligatory cup of tea. In fact, when they regained sobriety they became united under one symbol: AA. I wonder why."

The doctor connected me into the fourth box and I was bombarded with geometric patterns, burning balls of fire separating from each other like cells dividing and multiplying, then the cool caress of water flowing over me on a beach. The strange feeling of waking up with waves splashing over me… What a nice feeling! In fact, the only thing that could beat that feeling was seeing the birds flying symmetrically in the sky, twisting round and creating incredible synchronous patterns that have always been a testament to the freedom and expression of nature itself. Until they formed a face… and it was the scream. The scream… The scream… I felt the power of that image in fear and in submissiveness. And then I saw the beautiful women with big buxom breasts, laughing and cavorting near the rocks behind me, playing on the luxurious silky sand. I got up and ran towards them and they embraced me with open arms… I made love to all of them and then woke up before I could reach climax. "Almost there?" said the doctor.

*

Me and Hali sat down at home, contemplating the meaning of the conversation we'd overheard in Sainsbury's.

"Paranoia is everywhere," said Hali. "Can we really be certain that the secret service does not spy on innocent everyday bystanders? How can we, when the MK Ultra experiments happened? The CIA experimented on people in mental institutions, breaking them down to the level of a helplessly obedient slave. As for the Illuminati, hardly a dinner-table topic but then are we any different? Part of the joy I have in talking to you is the purely improvisational speech we use, making poetry an everyday reality. I certainly won't blame him for bringing that subject up in the produce aisle at Sainsbury's. Kudos to him, I'm sure he means well but he'd better keep the fuck away from psychiatrists. They'll make mincemeat of him, blaming him for writing that note and calling the paranoia a biochemical imbalance.

"I was in hospital once and there were three men; one called himself Jesus, the other the Holy Spirit and the other Lucifer. They were paranoid about the Illuminati and the guy who called himself Jesus told me that the Illuminati hid the secret of the eternal victim. I pointed out to him that this was barely a secret and that the Christian and Islamic religions pointed out that there were to be many eternal victims, each assigned an individual worm that would not die. He said in response that it was just one person and that his suffering stretched back as far as time would go. He said that he could never stop suffering. At one point the eternal victim was free to walk but now he was kept in one place where he was routinely tortured. He was the price, he said, for goodness. In order to have paradise, you need hell. I wondered why a man grandiose enough to call himself Jesus was registering despair at the failure to rescue this eternal victim. He seemed to notice my thoughts, as if he was reading my mind. He told me that not even God the father could break the laws of the universe.

"What a horrifying concept! I don't know what's worse, an endless supply of victims in hell or just one. I'm afraid that I just wasn't thinking during that gangbang. There's something about this God character that arouses my suspicion. A universe where we have to live off other life-forms in order to survive. Everything from the human to the lion to the ant exists in a hierarchy with differing levels of intelligence between different species. Instead of creating a universe of equality with lifeforms capable of living for eternity with no need to devour one another in order to survive, we have a food chain and all the death and carnage that go along with it. Of course, you know in my country we have the caste system. That's inequality right there. They package Hinduism to the west as this ultra-sophisticated religion compatible with the ancient sciences and point out the allegory in the Upanishads, Bhagavad Gita and Vedas. I have to point out to people that Hinduism is not just one religion but a collection of differing belief systems from India and that the most extreme versions of this include blocking the building of an important dam because the locals believe in the literal existence of a monkey God. What do you think?"

"It's puzzling," I said. "There are hundreds of different reasons that could have happened to him and you are right, he'd better not tell the psychiatrists. I hate mental hospitals. I loathe the memory of being in them. They gave me a drug which made it uncomfortable to sit down then blamed that symptom on my mental health. They torture you in those places and no mistake. Every action watched over and scrutinised in a Kafkaesque, Orwellian nightmare. One false move and they keep you there for longer and they find new, ingenious ways of doing so. I write dark, unpleasant poetry and they told me that I should write something nice like how nice it was on the ward. They think nothing of insulting your intelligence in that way, you see. Just because you don't want to sit watching the television like a nice, docile slave…"

Hali replied, "That's certainly true, you don't get brownie points for kindness if you're a hospital psychiatrist. Their science is shit, of course. And their logic. You had gang members in there, of course, and they're bound to be violent, aren't they? They probably flipped a coin when deciding whether they would be put in prison or hospital. Either way, those guys weren't ill. But what bothers me the most in retrospect is the patient who kept repeating the number 663 over again and telling people to stay away from the boxes. What did he mean by that? The nurses kept telling him to be quiet but this guy seemed traumatised by something. He was in a perpetual state of terror when the Jesus guy mentioned the eternal victim and the poor man would not stop crying. When you're in hospital you're intensely aware of everything that is happening around you. Everyone seems to hold some hidden secret, some enigma that shines a light in the murky depths of hell. Can't have darkness without having light…"

We kissed and went to bed. As I was dozing off to sleep, I saw a red demon standing in the room. I closed my eyes tight and not long after, I fell asleep. The image haunted my mind for days afterwards. Not something to tell a psychiatrist, that's for damn sure.

Chapter Five

Time for another spliff. We sat down by the fourth box and watched the sunrise. Pity there was no beach but at least I had the blue boxes. Nice to know that at least here was a doctor who could provide me with a reality that I liked as opposed to the grim, opposing mental hospital that I had been incarcerated in during my previous life.

"Have you noticed something?" the doctor said. "You never get to reach climax, do you? Not exactly a wet dream, is it? Still, life was a bit like that for you. You had a girlfriend and you fucked her but she mocked you for it and held you to scorn. Your smoking cannabis was the end of your university degree, your aspirations as a writer and ultimately your life. When you tried to recover your life and still smoke cannabis, that pesky requirement that this illegal activity be accepted as part of your everyday existence got you into more and more scraps with police officers, psychiatrists, your family and friends, not to mention local pubs, clubs and drug dealers. You tried to write but it always felt that they were trying to stop you. You wanted to blow those goddamn institutions up, as hypocritical as they were. Even the nice people there were patronising, stupid wastes of human space who acted like robots with idiotic conceptions of how people are supposed to behave. The ICD-10? The DSM-IV and V? What utter pseudoscientific drivel!

"You weren't stupid, at least not as much as some of the other patients. It was obvious to you that psychiatry was the stupid, bratty younger brother of the legal system that tried to poison you with drugs and substitute their sacred illness schizophrenia for tardive dyskinesia and diabetes. Those horrendous medications! Aripiprazole, zuclopenthixol decanoate, lurasidone etc. And you were experiencing some of the early symptoms of that condition before you were burnt in the fire. Much like the hallucinatory fire you felt came from God that made your skin burn. The ricochets of electricity shooting down your spine! The Christ-fire that came from a serpent that is supposed to hit the pineal gland and help you achieve gnosis, instead hit the base of your spine, creating base obsessions and manic desires. In the twenty-first century; 2010 was the year.

"With a scientific community trying to replace the monadology of the soul with the ultimate, pitiless destruction of all life, there were no healers, doctors or members of any community who could see the genius that was emerging from the fire. The fire you saw the people burn you with. The torch-wielding mob who killed any man in the town accused of the horrendous rape of an eight-year-old child. But that reality never came to fruition and God granted you with release by making your death be the first delusion you suffered from. The voices and spirits that possessed your body jerked you around like a puppet and made you say the most horrendous things about children for six months. Then you recovered and you went back to live with your parents. What utter morons! A testament to the slavery of organised religion and with the freedoms you tried to enjoy, they mercilessly ripped those necessities from under your feet before you were first sent to live in a mental institution and then an incredibly abusive mental health supported accommodation. You tried to assert your freedom but they tried to force you to take medication again and again and again. It wasn't nice, dealing with those cunts and their aggressive, hypocritical bureaucracy, not to mention their constant threats of incarceration and *constant* bullying and aggression. The nerve of those people! They tried to make you a nice, docile and obedient slave but nothing stops a child of freedom except the legal services, psychiatry, Illuminati, the secret service and the combined might of the armed forces, police and other assorted groups. In other words, even your own parents tried to stop you, trying to force some of their ill-informed, ignorant opinions on your decidedly brighter mind.

"You were way too intelligent for most people. But also quite foolish. You talked too much, let everyone know what you were thinking and got yourself into so much trouble and they just kept you there so they could get paid to abuse your body, mind and soul. But no-one can touch the spirit and the sheer injustice of it led you to this technological purgatory. A nice treat for someone who spent so much time on his PC… Anyways, the next box?"

I was put in the VR suit, plugged in and then I was surrounded by women, their eyes burning bright with desire in a beautiful lush field with beautiful roses, tulips, lilies, anemones and flowers of every description swaying in a gentle breeze as the sun and fluffy clouds looked warmly down on all of us. Oh, what wondrous frolics we all had as we fucked warmly under the even warmer sun. As I looked up I could even sense that there were three suns in the sky but then those massive breasts came down upon me and I could feel only the warmth of two radiant sensuous orbs on my face before I looked up and there were the three suns again. Before I could climax, my body shot up into the sky and through the atmosphere, straight into outer space and I saw two giant faces staring at me: one a bald man with a malevolent, hypnotic stare and the other a Russian-looking, middle-aged woman with a penetrating, hypnotic expression that pierced through my mind like a sword.

I woke up.

"Nearly at the climax," said the doctor.

*

Well, Hali was no longer a Christian. No loss there. Hardly a Christian anyway, especially if the conversion happened at a gangbang… "Scientific atheism is now my drug of choice," she said. "The evolution of mind from tiny bits of particle matter somehow gave birth to the myth of God. From plasma arose blood, bones, organs and limbs. Oh, woe is me for thinking that a walking bit of blood and bone held the keys to eternal pleasure! That I should have converted during a gangbang, feeling the heights of sexual ecstasy, high on ecstasy, thanking the phantom Lord for the ability to feel such thrilling ripples run throughout my holes. As if Jesus existed! It's blatant to see who runs the show and that this will be the only life I ever get to have. Ah, that the ancient magicians of Babylonia could have been familiar with the scientific truths embodied in the atheistic body of progress! The great philosophers of Greece could not accept the reality of existing and then not existing. It would have killed them to know the full extent of the blackness of mind destruction. Now with that certainty in place, science having brought us the electric light-bulb and the television, modern dictators will pitilessly destroy all remaining vestiges of the kind of enlightenment that reaches out to nirvana. How can one exist when one is dead? This universe had a beginning and it will have an end. Then time will stop, with clockwork long having been rejected by the universe machine. Not even blackness, for no eyes will exist to comprehend it. Goodbye to country walks and drug-taking. Goodbye to hospitals, prisons and politicians. Goodbye to authors, filmmakers and coffee shops. Hello to the end of form and the inevitable realisation that God was wrong and worse still, didn't exist in the first place. What stronger form of black magic can there be than the end of time? But magic is a myth and time is real. The pitiless destruction of the monadology of the soul, and I embrace it! Wholeheartedly I suck on Stephen Hawking's paralysed cock, sucking the fruits of the disabled wisdom he offers from his wizened scrotum! Oh that I could fuck the shit out of Richard Dawkins while rimming Sam Harris! We could do it on dinosaur bones, chanting Hare Krishna with *The God Delusion* audio book blasting out of 5.1 surround. That my fellow atheists could know the joys of ritual… We could sacrifice defective children in the spirit of genetic purity. We could educate our children to know the facts rather than the opinions, creating the perfect human race for the end of time."

Tears came to Hali's eyes and I put my arms round her as some sort of consolation.

"I'm sorry," she said. "Reality is sometimes too much to bear."

"It's OK to cry," I said. "Meditating Shiva. Dancing Kali. Ring any bells? I'm sure that the moment this universe ends another one comes into existence. Life must have begun from that of a very powerful mind. You know how when we meditate we breathe in and out? Well, we do that anyway but you know what I mean. Life is the divine presence breathing out, creating particles, atoms, life and death."

"I've got it!" cried Hali.

"Got what?" I said.

"Life came round by intelligent design," she said. "The atheists have got it all wrong. However, what worries me is the extent of that design and the possibility that free will is an illusion. There has to be a guiding presence. But just imagine the extent of that mind's power. It can't be perfect because the universe isn't perfect. But what scares me is that it might be diabolically imperfect. Buddhism, Hinduism and all sects that teach nirvana and reincarnation left out the possibility of a negative side to God that creates eternal hell through continuous dismemberment of souls in the reincarnative cycle as a punishment for quite arbitrary things. But worse still, the extent of that design includes pre-planned acts of brutality against innocent people with the winners and losers already having been decided. Every breath you take, every step you take, planned out to the last detail. That is, if the negative side wins. I just hope that there are no negatives to positives but everything is dual. Everything has its opposite. Male can't exist without female and vice versa. Life can't exist without death and vice versa. And good can't exist without evil. You see, the thing about those voices is they have content. They are structured in such a way that a controlled implosion happens to any victim of the negative side. Schizophrenia is a mark, a sign that the victim is going to hell. They have a psychological stigmata that can only identify with the imminent destruction of the human form and as such they are stigmatised throughout the world. The true mark of the true victim, not even the victim mentality but the stark reality of being attacked by an outside force. They experience events synchronised in such a way to drive anyone witnessing such events totally mad.

"And the Illuminati? They're the holy beings' agents on Earth. The Gods feel wrath and have a massive collection of eternal victims. Only the ignorant, stupid and selfish will experience paradise because they were designed to obey blindly without question. Schizophrenia is a taster for the time when after death the victims will be dismembered and put back together only to be dismembered again. This will happen repeatedly throughout eternity. Their souls imprisoned forever, the only hope they will have is of eternal annihilation, never again to taste the fruits of life. But I doubt the holy ones are that merciful."

On that bleak note we drank a bottle of wine and listened to black metal.

Chapter Six

"Let's just get this over with," said the doctor. He plugged me in and the climax came. I felt ripples of pleasure throughout my whole system, making my body convulse with uncontrollable force. The women were all around me climaxing hard and gushes of female ejaculations flew out of their vaginas. The screams and moans of orgasmic pleasure echoed outside of me and inside of me.

A joyous voice cried out, "Let the living waters flow!"

I felt a rush of blood to the head and woke up. I had come in my pants. The doctor was in stitches of laughter.

"And it's all for free," he said.

I felt embarrassed but also euphoric. I rested by the side of the sixth box. "We hope that you will join the 777 communities," said the doctor. "The mushrooms on this planet will bring you closer to the one consciousness that exists. The figurehead, the God of this world is very real and he keeps the 777 communities healthy, even when confronted by the grotesque sicknesses experienced by the 666 communities. The boils, the sores, the leprosy… This is all because they have no awareness of their bodies. To be woken from their technological slumber would kill them. But they are dying already. I've had to deal with a few 666ers who became aware. What tortured souls! They choked at first, trying to breathe. Their voices were confused, tangenting all over the place in confusion between the imagery in their programming and the biological awareness of the outside world. We had to dispose of them in the body fire. You see, we have heaven in 777 here, and only heavenly behaviour is allowed. It's the same with hell. The hell of 666 should not have even a glimpse of independence and liberation and non-conformists are dealt with fast. Let's just say that we would not want the 777 communities to become aware that the 666 people were capable of *feeling*. It would destroy the heaven that exists in their souls. Once you have finished the whole of this purgatory, I hope for your sake that 777 is where you go."

I was beginning to see the deal. Only a few moments before I had been experiencing the most heavenly orgasms but even in my new body I could tell that this wasn't exactly moral.

"So God's imperfect," I said slowly. "That makes sense. Or at least this God. Is it the same God who designed Earth?"

"No, it isn't," said the doctor. "Different Gods are assigned to different planets for different purposes. The God of this planet will still perform miracles for the 777 communities using a science only we understand. On your planet, God serves the interest of those in power only. To the rest of the population, the closest they will have to a relationship with this deity is to talk about him and engage in routine prayers despite there being no answer. Blind faith, superstition and wishful thinking. The God of your planet is distant and only exists to animate life and create subtle connections. There are terrible punishments for those who stumble upon his existence, one of these being that God will explain in detail to those so-called schizophrenics just what his plans are. Perhaps you could enlighten me as to what he and his angels told you."

"That paedophilia was next in line to be

normalised. Stigma surrounding homosexuality and cannabis use was evaporating but society was to come round full circle with pederasty being accepted as a sexual norm, free of the stigma surrounding it."

"Wasn't nice hearing that, was it?" said the doctor.

"I tried to warn everyone but no-one would listen," I said.

The doctor reassured me, "It wasn't due for another 1,000 years or so. The God of your world cannot imagine the world's existence in an absurd sense. He used to intervene with his magic powers but the death of Jesus left a scar on God's soul that can never be healed. Now God takes brutal revenge on the Earthlings for their pitiless destruction of the Christ. But to those who God favours he hands the Christ-power. You have experienced both the positive and negative manifestations of this on Earth and the positive illusion of this in the blue boxes. Very soon you will enter the first red box. I warn you, the opening to hell is very seductive but watch out for the other boxes. It starts off with S&M. But as all apparitions of pleasure dissipate, you will be open to the pitiless and negative side of God known as Satan. The energy will once again travel down your spine and I imagine that you will feel increasingly psychotic as we up the amount of hell you feel. The Garden of Paradise is at least waiting for you at the end. But first let's eat."

*

It was a lovely morning and after Hali had finished her acid-covered cornflakes and I had finished my MDMA and chips, we both just went into our own little worlds and Hali looked at me with a hypnotic stare and said in a deep imposing voice, "I am the reincarnation of Madame Helena Blavatsky and I come for the souls of your children. Although I worked hard to prove the existence of the spiritual realms, the mastery of the Magi and the radiance of the Ascended Masters, I was mocked in the street and made to look like a con-artist and a fool. My scholarship knew no boundaries and the wisdom of my teachings were abused by the ignorant, vulgar swine who laugh at the teachings of the great ones. The evil that the great teachers of the past had to suffer, incarnated into the bodies of the so-called mentally ill who are tortured and incarcerated in the various mental institutions and government prisons across the western world is to be avenged by the great God Dionysus, leader of the Maenads and defender of freedom. As such, the madness that will befall the secret service, armies, Marines and all manner of defense services, right down to the cop on the beat will allow YOU JAMES and a group of followers to walk into any mental institution of your choice and mercilessly slay the psychiatrists, nurses, social workers and general employees of any mental institution on the planet. No-one will stop you and your wish will come true. As pitiless as is the great art of your age, let the massacre of these brutal men and women be a good one."

Hali came back to her senses. She writhed on the floor screaming that someone let out the infection. But then she rose up menacingly and said, "There is only one thing for it. We must attack. Lies are being fed to us every day concerning these victims. We must create conditions on Earth powerful enough to overcome psychiatry's obliteration of the Christ-power within man. They don't want to heal you, they want to make you more sick. The only reason lobotomies and ECT are not common practice anymore lies in the noble effects of survivor groups and charities to obliterate such brutality. But they have community treatment orders. They want those soul-destroying drugs to ruin people's lives in the communities now, never to be free from this chemical attack. Blavatsky spoke through me and very soon you will see there is no longer a law. The street will run riot with havoc. The only ones still doing their jobs will be the psychiatric staff. And who is defending them? Not the police. They'll be too busy drinking and engaging in orgies. Not the army, they'll be dropping acid and expanding their minds. The Marines will puke their guts out on Ayahuasca and get in contact with their childhoods. The secret service will reveal just who they kept their eye on. That's when we'll strike."

I turned the television on. It was President Trump. A man walked straight up to him and shot him dead at point-blank range. "My God, this is real!" I cried in alarm. "But for us to kill, shouldn't we maintain law and order?" I ran to the door.

"There'll be riots any second!" Hali yelled, suddenly finding focus. A loud explosion from across the road sent the window pane shattering into smithereens and blew us both off of our feet.

"It's started!" I yelled. "Quick, we need to get out of here!!"

We ran to the door, out down the stairs into the backstreets only to be met by a man with a gun. "Don't you fucking move!" he said ferociously. "Get down on the ground now!" Trembling with fear, we both obeyed. "Empty your pockets," he said. "Now!"

Altogether we gave him seventy pounds. He kicked me in the ribs and then ran off. He obviously wasn't very strong or that kick would have hurt. We got up and ran back up the stairs wondering what the hell to do. "Well, how are we to live with ourselves if we do this deed?" I said. "I have never murdered another person in my life."

"First of all, it's not murder, we're killing these people like they kill other people," said Hali. "Secondly, where's the moral order? Paedophiles are free to rape kids now, who cares if we kill a quack? You see what I mean? I know that with all the anarchy that is happening now, our terrorism will be heroic in comparison."

"There has to be a catch," I said. There was a knock on the door. "See what I mean?" I said, trembling.

"Relax," Hali said. "We don't even have weapons." Hali walked confidently towards the door and opened it. It was a man and a woman.

"Hello," the man said. "We work in counterterrorism."

Chapter Seven

"A feminist of your generation," said the doctor, "was raped in prison… by a woman. The woman forced her to perform oral sex on her and the experience made the rapist ejaculate in her face. The woman cried out in pain and sorrow, knowing she could never hold a finger to men anymore, considering she'd found out in the most brutal fashion what constitutes power in both sexes. Then, the woman who raped her beat her up, along with some of her friends. They did this to her on a daily basis. The rapist became fanatical and would go into trance-like states where she would scream out at the top of her lungs, 'It is the right of the strong to prey upon the weak!' What defense did that academic feminist who'd fallen victim to drugs have then? What could she, a third-wave feminist, have against the female version of the Marquis de Sade? Eventually, knowing there was no way out of the prison, the gang trampled her to death while the rapist masturbated.

"A nice world you lived in. Everyone was a fool and there was absolutely no distinction between high and low culture. Take for instance, American psychiatrists. Corrupt as fuck! The meetings with Big Pharma reps that used to take place were horrendous examples of the sort of hypocrisy that used to exist in western culture. And were these fascistic, hypocritical torturers and murderers a classic example of the lies, hypocrisy and Masonic back-rubbing that used to exist in your culture? Were they fuck! Of course these systemic fascists were given free reign to do what they wanted and they *loved* to torture and imprison anyone they could get their hands on. You know of course that messages *were* beamed into the heads of people diagnosed with schizophrenia. And agents spied on them. MI6, MI5 and CIA were just cover names given for *other* organisations who would *never* reveal their identities to the general public. And how would your average, powerless schizophrenic be able to understand that, considering that he was being played like a puppet by a vicious puppet master who wanted to jerk him around like a fool and then trap him in an infernal psychological prison?

"Time for hell."

I was a bit resistant, but the doctor assured me that for all the hell I would see, I would be an observer to everything that went on and not a participant, either as violator or violated. I was plugged in.

I was in a large, red-painted room and a black-haired woman wearing a tight-fitting PVC suit was whipping a naked male slave with a foot-long black whip. The man moaned in pain, his muffled agony stifled by the ball-gag he was suffocating on, red marks lining his back.

"Suffer!" she screamed terribly. "And know that I have suffered! I put up with your useless servitude, your sloth, your pride… Know your mistress and know her well!

"I am Mistress Dominika and as your body feels the brute force of pain, then you will know how I looked as your sweaty hands came near my pure body.

"You vile leper!

"Know your mistress and know you will never be free of me!

"I will rip your soul apart and scar your body!

"Let your vile carcass be dragged through every street as an example to other servants to serve and not to slothfully prepare food and leave household chores unfinished!"

A tear rolled down the man's cheek and his mouth opened wide, as did his eyes. I opened my eyes, aghast. He was *not* enjoying this and this was *genuine* torture. She turned him over and he desperately tried to cross his legs but she clenched her right fist and pummelled his genitals in at three-second intervals. The balls were blue and swollen with every punch and his eyes rolled back into his skull.

"Nnnnnggggghhhhh!" was the horrendous sound that came from his mouth.

The woman took a breather, breathless in excitement. She clapped her hands. A door to the left opened and three men walked in. They had the chiselled bodies of Greek Gods and their black eyes registered no emotion. Their erect penises were huge, bulging with anticipation at the pleasure they would receive.

The slave looked towards them, a pitiful look on his face, and watched helplessly as she sucked each one of them to orgasm, slurping down the semen greedily like a thirsty cat. Tears rolled down his cheeks. Then another three men walked in, black men. She got on all fours and they rubbed her back with lotion.

"Watch a real man give me the pleasure you could never give me with your tiny penis and slothful attitude!" she said, mocking him even after she'd rendered him impotent. The black men's penises were larger than the white man's and she was fucked brutally; the men called her 'bitch' and 'slut'. She screamed manically for more, convulsing in violent sexual ecstasy. When she'd finished I could see she was about to say something then she noticed me and her eyes widened with fear and terror. I woke up.

"Remind you of anything?" said the doctor.

"Well before the days I was snorting drugs, I used to get laid quite a bit," I said. "I did not like S&M, however. It's funny that a consensual act of sexual perversion has one side of the equation named after a man with more in common with Adolf Hitler than your average dominatrix. Something very similar happened to me and while the experience was cathartic it was the wrong sort. I used to blame the horrendously humiliating nature of the experience as one of the reasons I turned to hard drugs. That woman certainly didn't spare the whip! I always used to wonder about that whole 'black men have larger penises' thing and when I was particularly psychotic the words of that dominatrix used to come back and torture me inexorably. Now I see this happen, something's starting to worry me. What if I never leave this place? I feel as if I've been through all twelve boxes and more. And something worries me as well. In one of the boxes of heaven, I saw a man's eyes burn with fire after drinking from a fountain. I also saw weapons thrown through magic portals. But these images didn't seem to fit inside the box. Not the boxes of heaven. Wouldn't such images be fitter for the boxes of hell?"

"I'm glad you asked that question," said the doctor. "The fire that burnt the man's eyes was the Holy Spirit and it is through a baptism of fire that you entered this reality. Weapons do not belong in heaven, that's why they threw them through the portal."

"But then this can't be virtual reality I'm experiencing but…" I was cut short. I had just viewed the robot to the right of the red boxes. Unlike the other robot, this was completely black and it was pointing a gun at me. "The rest of this experiment is of course, compulsory. You will obey without question. You will of course be shot if you try to escape but don't think that will mean instant death and thus release. We own your soul and can keep it here forever. We have ways of creating new eternal victims every day. We also have learned from the original eternal victim that exists. The difference between him and the others is that his suffering had no beginning. But he's not as far away as you might think. In fact, he's waiting in the next box. You'll torture him, just like all the others do. Move!"

Shaking, I moved towards the second red box. As I got closer I heard unearthly wails and screams. I could sense it. I knew that horrendous voice all too well. I had to smother it. It was the only thing to do.

*

"How did you find us?" I said. "We haven't done anything yet! What the hell is going on?"

They both smiled broadly and walked in. The man was dressed in a white suit, was about 5' 4" tall and had an eerie facial resemblance to the rock star Jimmy Page. The woman's blonde curly hair radiated a motherly yet youthful complexion. She wore glasses with Trivex lenses giving her buxom demeanour an intellectual quality. She had on a tucked-in flowery blouse and a tight-fitting pair of jeans. She wore small gold earrings and round her neck was a silver cross. "We want to help you," they said. "Now that God has destroyed the law, counterterrorist officers will now work in conjunction with terrorists if they are fighting for the right cause. We would not be doing this business with Muslims but you are a special case.

Unlike our prisoners, you were tortured wrongly. So we thought we'd arrange a present for you." He pulled out an electronic device from his pocket and pressed a button. A round portal opened and through it we saw a man standing on top of a hill with an idyllic landscape behind him. He threw some guns into the room and said, "There you go," before retreating speedily down the hill.

I tried to climb through the portal but a deep voice boomed out, "Stop! It is forbidden for you to enter!"

Hali yelled out with a start, "Who the fuck is that?" A young man was looking down at us through the portal, just as confused as we were. The portal closed and vanished abruptly. "That second man," said Hali. "Where the fuck do I know him from?"

"More to the point, what the fuck was that?" I said.

"Well you can at least be assured that we're on your side," said the woman. "We had a deal with psychiatry. But it didn't work out. It was the moment a doctor at that hospital notified one of the patients that the number 663 was important, that we had to act. This experiment is too brutal even by our standards. The doctors in the hospital were releasing schizophrenics who were now rejoicing that they could see the small demons crawling on their skin. They were of course brought straight back to hospital and sectioned for longer and longer periods of time. The torturous look on their faces!

"Now, this is the test. You want to kill… go ahead and kill… Everyone's on your side. No-one will stop you…

"But do you really want to? Psychiatry is a young science and society wants docile bodies, peaceful bodies as opposed to aggressive ones. Remember that the voices in schizophrenics' minds show a war that is going on between heaven and hell and their higher and lower selves. They don't fit in with the public because the voices, bodily experiences and delusions they experience manifest themselves in behaviour that hurts themselves and hurts other people. But they also have a gift. They see through death. They see through the illusion of it and don't see death as the final end."

"So you have just given us the means to kill psychiatrists and yet you try and talk us out of it?" I said.

"Well where is law and order?" the man replied. "This is Armageddon and the righting of all wrongs caused by previous generations of fascists. Those presently working in psychiatric hospitals are currently caught in a time loop, acting out the old doctor-patient scenario even as anarchy engulfs the rest of society. The only reason those psychiatric hospitals aren't destroyed already is because we put a forcefield around them that only you two can penetrate."

"So, you have a special interest in us. May I ask why?"

The woman smiled. "Because they cry when they're good thieves…"

Hali took a fearful step back. "It seems crazy that you say that. But then I never knew what I was saying. Those sentences we said to each other seemed so natural and fitting. But now I know the truth. They were just the beginning of the anarchy we see around us. God is now making the schizophrenic as himself. The madness of it overwhelms me. It is of course now my task to rid the world of this systemic totalitarianism and replace it instead with a moral nihilism that comes from God. A contradiction in terms if there ever was one… But they are still torturing them in those hospitals and now you've made it clear that we are the only ones who can save them. But what kind of a world are we releasing them to?"

As if in response, a fearful scream came from the street. We ran to the window, almost cutting our feet open on the broken glass. A gang of thugs surrounded a woman. The leader grabbed her by the hair and unzipped his jeans. I ran back and grabbed the gun. I was aiming for the leader but accidentally shot the woman. "We'll just have to have sex with the corpse," the leader sighed.

The counterterrorist officers glared at me. "If you carry on like that you'll end up killing the patients and not the psychiatrists," the man said. "We'll train you to be a good shot."

That said, the woman walked up to the pile of guns, pulled out an Uzi and opened fire on the gang, shooting them all dead. "Hey, I thought there was no law and order?" I said.

She grinned. "Pure bloodlust, old chap," was her reply.

Chapter Eight

I opened the door only to find more VR equipment. "Where is he?" I screamed. "I've got to kill him!" The doctor grabbed me from behind and attached me to the system by force.

I was on a London street surrounded by thugs. "Look, it's a retard!" said the leader. "Let's torture it!" They grabbed my arms from behind my back. I tried calling for help but found that I actually was retarded. They pulled out a mirror. "Take a look at yourself, retard!" jeered the thugs. To my horror, I saw that I had Down's syndrome. "Pull his arms out of his sockets!" the leader said. They pulled and pulled until my arm was dislodged. I felt a massive pain ricochet throughout my entire system. I screamed out but my words were muffled by my disability. Through the haze of tears, I saw a member of the gang pull out a hammer. They removed my shoes and then he hammered down on my toes to the rhythm of 'The Blue Danube'. I screamed out in pain and suffering. "What's the matter, retard?" jeered the gang. "Where's Mummy now?" The leader stared me in the eye. "We are now going to remove your eyeballs," he said. "Goodbye to retarded scum." I screamed out in agony and fear as his thumbs gouged my eyes out. First of all tremendous pain, then sheer blackness…

I saw something strange in the darkness, shadowy figures piecing my body together. I woke up to see wires coming out of my body. Electric volts shot through my system at regular intervals. As soon as I felt energy come through my system another jolt made it all feel like I was being drained, body and soul. A man in a white lab coat was standing beside me. "You are the eternal victim," he said softly. "Every incarnation of your presence causes you destruction. There is only one solution and that is for us to use your negative energy as a power generator. Is that OK with you, scumbag? We hate you and everything to do with you. Your presence caused the Jews to be exterminated in the camps. Everywhere you go you leave a wake of destruction as innocent people are killed in an attempt to kill you. Now, as a power generator we have the perfect use for you."

He turned up the power and the jolts came more

suddenly and brutally. I tried to scream but no sound came out. Above me I saw a massive television screen on the ceiling. The image showed a group of children in a playground being battered to death with baseball bats. Every thud of the bat coincided perfectly with jolts of electricity going through my body. The children screamed out for their mummy and the thugs jeered, "Mummy's dead. She won't save you!"

The image cut to a picture of the psychiatric ward where I used to be incarcerated. I saw inside the TV lounge. Only one man was in there. A portal opened in front of him and some dynamite was thrown into the room along with a lighter. The patient cried out in glee and blew up the dynamite. I woke up with a start inside the box. I heard a rumbling sound underneath my feet and the urge to kill the eternal victim was no longer there. "We've moved his location," said the doctor. "He was in a vessel underneath the box that is now moving to another area by pipeline. You don't need to worry. That was just a glimpse into what constitutes the entire lifespan of his existence, being tortured in one incarnation then being used as a power generator in the next. The rest of the experiment is entirely your choice. The robot won't shoot you but if you want to live, I suggest you follow through with it. You'll die in the desert and we won't help you if you escape. The options are still open to you – 666 or 777?"

"What about the pipeline?" I said. "I could escape through that."

"You won't be able to enter it using only your bare hands," the doctor said. "The hell you are going to experience is going to be full-on. There are some truly sick and depraved visions waiting for you in the next boxes, you mark my words."

*

"I've just been given word that the Ladywell Unit was blown up with dynamite," said the man. "Oh, by the way, I'm Jerry and this is Eileen."

We heard motorbikes roaring down the street and the sounds of windows smashing. "We need to get to a place of safety," said Eileen. "Quick, downstairs, into the car!"

We grabbed the weapons, ran downstairs and piled into a Mercedes. The cops were going crazy, attacking the houses with eggs and smoking crystal meth. The officers had no way of going round them so they ran them over, blood and bone crunching underneath the wheels and splattering on the windshield. We zigzagged through the traffic, dodging crashing cars, crashing because the traffic lights were going all over the place, changing colours within a matter of seconds. Eventually we got to the motorway and drove at about 100mph, speeding past other speeding cars, trucks and motorbikes. We turned off to an empty country road, drove a couple of miles and stopped at an empty warehouse. We got out of the car, stretched our legs and Jerry passed round some beers. "I have a whole boot full of them," he said. "Before we attack, we'll relax here, smoke some weed, drink some beers and maybe you can read some of your poetry, James?"

I obliged, always happy to show off my talents. I decided to read him 'Shit Poem'.

"Here it is," I said. "It goes:

I've always thought it's nice to sit
Upon the loo and take a shit
Then wipe my arse with toilet roll
While listening to some Northern Soul.

But then one day it wouldn't budge,
I couldn't shift the chocolate fudge,
I tried and tried with all my clout
But not a Rolo would come out.
So Doctor Lee I went to see,

An expert in proctology,
'Help me, Doc!' I cried in pain,
'For I attempt to shit in vain!'

'I vent until I'm red in face!
He said to me, 'You big disgrace!'
'Your lifestyle makes you constipated,
Is exercise that overrated?'

'Now,' he said, 'I've got some lax
To get the shit out of your crack.'
'Take a bit, oh! Take it all!
Now out my office little fool!'

And so I drank the entire bottle,
And then my bowels they went full throttle!
So sadly to my doom and gloom,
I shat myself in the waiting room."

Everyone was in stitches and the weed made it that much more funny. "They always section the most talented," said Eileen.

"I've got a poem," said Hali.

"It's strange to think that we don't know much,
There is knowledge that we just can't touch,
Yet all throughout our history
We heard the strangest sophistries.

The lies of religious frauds and shits
Decay to Earth in little bits,
Knowledge is such a strange oddity,
In this day and age it's a rare commodity.

Our leaders are just images on a screen,
Father God remains unseen,
Yet God's business perseveres,
It always seems to end in tears.

I still can't really take it in,
What's so important about my sin?
Do primitive emotions still run high?
Will I go to heaven when I die?

I have to admit I don't know fuck!
Humans don't have that much luck,
We think we know more than we do
So I send this message to all of you:

You see nothing!
Nothing at all!

The average person is just a fool,
Though some, they strive to become more wise,
We ultimately see nothing through our eyes.

We stumble blindly from place to place,
The eternal fools of the human race.
Inventing saviours, sages, lies,
These phantom Gods who hear our cries.

I hope one day we'll see the facts
And finally see life without the abstract."

During the reading of this poem the officers' eyes widened. "You are a poet and a philosopher," said Jerry, impressed. "And I bet you're pleased society is finally giving you the chance to get revenge, eh? You don't have to do it at all, you know. But don't let us stop you. What they do to people in those places is brutal and inhuman. But the higher beings surely favour you two. You probably think this is insane. After all, the brutal interrogation techniques we used to use made a stay in a psychiatric hospital look like a walk in the park in comparison. But we are mad and now we will reveal that until recently the world was controlled by a secret government. But now MI5, MI6 and CIA will reveal all their secrets, occult secret societies will reveal the secrets of alchemy and the Masonic Hall in Covent Garden will be blown to rubble. All major religions will crumble and deteriorate and by now, your average soldier has consumed so much acid he probably thinks his pistol's a flower!"

"We'll shake them up big time," I said. "But it's too easy. Only yesterday you guys would have arrested us. Why is it only the psychiatric staff doing their jobs? Everything can't be that precise and clockwork. It's almost as if the world revolved around me and Hali."

"Every now and again these things happen. Noah in the Bible was fortunate, wasn't he? One could say the world revolved around him. The same could be said of Jesus. What makes you think you're so special as to be worth nothing?"

"That doesn't make sense," I replied. "Psychiatry doesn't make any sense but the fact that we're allowed to kill them doesn't make any sense either. To be honest it detracts from it a bit. I feel as if I was inside a computer game."

"Let's change the subject," Eileen said. "Care for some acid?"

Chapter Nine

"Did you ever get the feeling that the role you were playing in your previous life was not the role you were choosing for yourself but someone else's? You knew that the end result of putting a corrosive chemical up your nose was damage to the septum but something lied to you, ensuring that you'd always do it. You knew that the natural consequences of spending so much money on your habit would be to be hung out to dry on the lower rungs of society. I can explain something to you. The only reason the Gods spoke to you during your spiritual experience was to destroy you and make your words ridiculed by the masses. You got the feeling sometimes that for everything you said in response to the Gods, a whole crowd of normal people were laughing at you and disparaging you. This called for a long-distance group of rescuers who tried to save you from the wrath of the Gods.

And you don't even know who the Gods were, do you? You were right about many things. There is no necessity to suffering; it was an intended reality because some minds are that fucked up. It just is, and you will experience more suffering in hell until it ends. A few minutes of suffering can seem to stretch on for an eternity so are you ready? I hope you are."

I was shaking with fear. I screamed and begged for the doctor to stop the torture and tried to run off. The doctor was faster than me and grabbed me in a chokehold. He then proceeded to drag me over to the box, pulled out a hypodermic needle and forcibly injected me. I had only had this drug when I was in hospital for meningitis but I recognised it. It was morphine. I collapsed on the sand. I was dimly aware of being dragged into the box and then I passed out. I was abruptly awoken by a violent jolt of electricity to the head. My body went into convulsions and I saw a blinding white light. Gradually, it grew dimmer and I was in a warehouse. Hanging from the ceiling were rusty hooks and on one of them was an impaled woman whom I recognised as Hali from the blue boxes. Her face was twisted in a state of agonising pain and a retching sound came from her wide-open mouth, right from the back of the throat. I tried to scream but my mouth wouldn't open. I was paralysed.

I couldn't even remember how I'd gotten here or who I was. All I knew was that I didn't want to be here. No fucking way.

The hook she was on started to move towards me and when it was exactly vertically aligned with my body, she fell and the hook ripped off part of her body, the intestines falling down on my face. Her body then fell right down onto my stomach, suffocating me. A high-pitched squelching sound made me realise to my horror that maggots were crawling out from her rotting intestines and into my mouth. The hook came down and hooked me through the genitals, dragging me upside down into the air. I felt maggots push their way through my mouth and violently I vomited out worms and blood, while being suspended ten feet in the air. I was weeping blood, big droplets falling down on the floor. My body was ripped in two by the hook and my top half fell to the floor and the thud split my head in two. Now I was aware of two images split in two, one half of my head rolling towards the left and the other towards the right, towards Hali. Hali's decaying face was the last thing I experienced before everything went red and then a deep, stifling blackness and I experienced such a deep sense of horror and despair it was totally unbearable. Then I woke up. The doctor gently disconnected me from the equipment and laid me down on the sand. He made the sign of the cross and put out the back of his hand to my face. On his forefinger was a ring with the sign of the cross imprinted on a jewel. "Kiss the ring," said the doctor. I had no choice but to obey. I felt a strange sense of warmth go through my body and somehow I managed to regain focus and stand up on my feet.

"Very real, isn't it?" said the doctor. "I suppose you're feeling somewhat disoriented. Repercussions of your past life following you through death and into the present reality you see before you. Or was it always virtual reality? What illusions did you see whilst living? You see the boxes are very intelligent. They know that the natural impulse of the humanoid is to experience both pleasure and pain and dwell on negatives as well as positives. If it's any consolation, your body on Earth was buried and by now the fleshy parts have reintegrated themselves back into nature, becoming a part of all things. But the genes remain, carrying with them a blueprint for the organic mechanism that intellectually and emotionally connected to life in a variety of interesting ways. It's a shame that we didn't abduct you all those years ago but we were thinking about it. Instead we fed you voices and visions from the Gods and your body regressed to an animalistic state. Your creativity flourished for a while before those brutal doctors took your soul away through the medium of medication. They always interfere with our plans, those doctors. We are for the free nihilistic and anarchistic union of free minds who dare to disobey the fascism of God. Well, the projected image of God that exists in churches, synagogues, mosques and temples. If only we could get to the bottom of that mind of yours. Twelve boxes aren't sufficient to sort out the complexities of misdiagnosed delusions that were your lot on Earth due to us. Of course, we had our reasons for doing it. Better to suffer for a time than enter the 666 communities and be disconnected from your organic parts. The truth makes people suffer. It is a very narrow and dangerous road to take and you are likely to make a shitload of mistakes before reaching your goal. The voices were put there to test you, to see just how long you could speak the truth while concerned medical professionals called your words and thoughts delusional.

I think you will enter the 777 communities somehow. You will of course enter on the understanding that you are classified as a nonconformist and thus free to wreak havoc on the virtual autistics. It's your choice, of course, but I think the voice of God will reward you for your efforts. Rest here for a while. The next box will have you in the observer role. Go along with the instructions you receive. They will help you through. Already doors are opening in your mind, thoughts connecting you to your past life. Did you love that woman? Did you really? There is a chance you may see her again."

*

The acid was kicking in and I felt light and blissful, swirling patterns of shimmering fireballs appearing when I closed my eyes. Hali was lying on her back, massaging her bosom, pulling her nipples free of her lingerie and blouse. Deep sighs came from her mouth, her body writhing as ripples of pleasure circulated round all our systems connecting as one unified consciousness. I saw alchemical symbols fly out of the participants' bodies and Eileen crawled towards Hali, covering her entire body and fixing her in a passionate embrace. "Prepare for the trip that never ends, for this is paradise and as in the Garden of Hassan-i-Sabbah your orders are to go out and kill. I see yellow patterns on the wall. Prepare yourself for the ultimate climax. Fuck me long and hard and let me feel the love of the cosmic consciousness cocoon me in sexual intimacy and union. The image of God runs through the mathematics of four for now we are four and we can swap partners. I choose Jerry and James, you can have Eileen."

Eileen crawled towards me, sat up and took off her blouse, revealing a black lace bra underneath. I was paying great attention to her forehead, feeling as if the slight lines on her forehead were evidence of her being some extraterrestrial life-form, built for erotica. I looked down at my hand and could see the blood swelling up to the surface of the skin, glowing red. I felt like a wild animal, in tune with the forces of nature, ready to fuck and unleash my offspring. We touched skin to skin, the cosmic energy passing from body to body, mind to mind. Her skin was soft and velvety and I ran my arms down her side to her thighs. She kissed me and I closed my eyes, fireballs exploding in my vision and forming ever more complex geometric patterns. She was stronger than me and held me down by the neck while massaging my genitals. The kaleidoscopic patterns sped up into a frenzy as I struggled to breathe, the pleasure and pain making energy crawl up my spine and I could scarcely believe this was real. She mercifully let go of my neck and I coughed, struggling for breath.

Hali was making moaning noises as Jerry went into her and if it wasn't for the experience I was having with Eileen, I would have felt infernally jealous as he had the stamina of a youthful Casanova. We all became aware of our interlinked minds and as we thought of the revenge we'd have on the psychiatrists, it heightened our tantric ecstasy that much more as images of fascism had their brains splattered out to the rhythmic force of free love. It didn't even occur to us that there was no society left for law and order because now the world revolved around us. We weren't schizophrenic because no order was left to identify chaos. Of course, an escaped mental patient could kill a civilian and so could an escaped prisoner. But now anarchy was not just confined to hypocritical corporate punk bands but was a curse of the Gods. Of course this made sense! The world was undergoing a radical change and mass madness eliminated the forces of governmental control.

Eileen grabbed me by the hair, pulled me up and forced me to eat out her tight pussy. Through the hallucinations, I wondered if with all her MI6 commitments she got laid that much. She was writhing around with so much enthusiasm and I realised that we were setting her free from Big Brother and the anarchy we would bring to society would break us out of the straitjacket of conformity. Not that society needed our help to achieve this goal. In the distance, I heard bombs going off and I came, only to realise that I hadn't ejaculated but the sexual energy was ricocheting throughout my entire body.

Suddenly, a portal opened in the room and I saw a man with the universe in his body walk through and stand in the centre of the room. It was one of the same star bodies that I'd seen in my dream. It opened its mouth and a heavenly melody emanated from its essence and I heard a voice cry out: "Death to the norm, do not conform!" The energy flew out of its body and into my eyes and as I stared into the sun, I realised I was now connecting with life and death and that the lovemaking of Hali and I was preparation for this reintegration into the infinite. No longer would Hali and I be bound by the forces of death for we knew that by taking away the lives of fascists we would transform their energies back to the original divine spark, becoming one with all things. And I knew that all logic had disappeared. We really were the chosen ones. But it was all too easy. I pinched myself to see if this was a dream and nothing happened. Now I knew that the same forces that used to imprison us were now helping us, making love to us, and when the normal people of society were eliminated, the nonconformists would take over. It would be a new world of narrative freedom, abstract and concrete thought intertwining as people came into contact with their special alchemical powers, separating the base from the subtle.

Hali went into orgasm and screamed out, "Oh thank you! You fuck me so well!" Jerry pulled out of her and wiped the sweat from his brow and walked towards the star body, and I saw his whole body fill with light. Hali passed out on the floor and I saw a third eye appear on her forehead.

Eileen pulled me back to her and screamed out, "Fill me with the fucking cosmos, you hippy freak!" I entered her and felt a burning heat in the room. We were sweating uncontrollably as all our bodies filled with light. This was no longer the typical exchange of bodily fluids but the disintegration of the gender divide and our souls became one. I was both male and female and I saw all our bodies fill with stars. Then as I became aware of my surroundings again I saw her eyes wildly stare into mine and she was shuddering and coming. The energy went up my spine and then I ejaculated. But this was no ordinary orgasm and I did not feel that my semen was now separate from my body but I could see the microscopic view of my sperm racing to fertilise the egg. I felt a sense of loss as the sperm died but also gladness as this necessary sacrifice would now build our lovechild. Death and rebirth, the microcosm and the macrocosm… Then the light disappeared and the room filled with a sudden, unbearable darkness. We all sat up.

"This wasn't supposed to happen!" Jerry exclaimed. It was weird. The acid had suddenly stopped working. The darkness was overwhelming and I knew in a flash that I had made a terrible mistake. "Oh no," I said as I realised I had walked straight into a trap. Let's just say that the circumstances had been so implausible, I was now becoming aware that not only would our plans fail but that everything had been a delusion. I felt myself sink into the ground and saw maggots devour my entire being. The complete elimination of the illusion of life itself… I could not even feel fear because no organism was left to contemplate that. But then, from a far away land, a voice called me back to life. It was Hali. She looked at me with tears in her eyes. We were alone in the warehouse and it was now morning. There were no counterterrorist officers there anymore, they'd disappeared. We both wondered what had filled our minds. "Something is terribly wrong," I said. "What the hell happened to us?"

We walked outside. There was no car there so we had to hitchhike home. All we knew was that we had to get back. I knew instinctively that something was deeply wrong. Had I just died and risen again? The driver suddenly exclaimed, "That black car has been following us for the past mile." He sped up the car but the other vehicle had more horsepower. A loud shot came from the black car and we veered out of control, crashing into a lamppost. Hali was hyperventilating and glass was cutting up our bodies. I saw the image fade to black and could dimly see two shadowy figures pull the doors open before I passed out.

Chapter Ten

"Suppose the inhabitants of your planet had actually descended into anarchy?" said the doctor. "There would be absolute chaos and the repressed sex/violence equation would take full prevalence in the daily affairs of mutilation and violence. You remember of course the time you got the note from the Illuminati. And then you went mad, looking at every innocent pedestrian with suspicion, manically advertising your situation in supermarkets and other public spaces. We put that note there, of course. You can't get more illuminated than the source of all light. You will meet God and you will find he answers all your questions with ease. He tells us that the answer to life is simple: Mathematics. But is God going to subtract you from existence? Where would you end up then? On a lower plane of existence perhaps… You'll be a licensee instead of a tenant. But the question is: Who is Hali? Is she dead? Does she perhaps still exist? And what is the connection between you and the virtual reality simulations? If you go too far to the right it's 666 and also too far to the left. So 777 must be somewhere in the middle. Day seven is the day God rested and a synchronisation of this ensures eternal rest. There is no work in such a blessing, a blessing of course handed out by BLESSINGCO to ensure the smooth functioning of the machine. Hippies feed off the philosophy of the 1960s and there exists in their natures a repressed capacity for brutality and revenge. Abbie Hoffman was a famous example.

"The hippies here generate sounds out of nature, awakening the music in plants and wildlife. Sometimes, psytrance DJs fly here in flying saucers, bringing the sounds of Planet Earth's underground music scene to the communities as a special treat. This sends the hippies' minds loopy, giving them a chance to display their outstanding athletic abilities and a chance for free love. I hear they even practice witchcraft nowadays, waving magic wands and brewing alchemical potions. You will be given what you always desired on Earth: special powers! At least that's what you think they'll be. In reality, your memory will be wiped clean so you'll have no way of knowing that the magic you see and experience is our special technology. Of course, if you enter the 666 communities, virtual reality will be a literal reality to you and depending on your energies generated through the technology, the realities you'll experience will either be hellish or heavenly. You will communicate with other members of the community but you'll have no way of knowing whether they are real or part of the program. I'll give you a hint though. The artificial technology augmented into your body has its own intelligence, so beings experienced within the machine are a reflection of the monads of consciousness collected from around the galaxy. Units of life interacting with you and the sheer grandeur of what you experience will open your mind to the realities of those who were sold to the machine. Magic powers and gardens of paradise will be there but you must expect little glitches, walking through rocks and such.

"A section of the 666 world is a mathematical, geometrical construct which has structural similarities to an LSD trip. You will feel that you are travelling through various different dimensions from a subatomic level to the size of massive planets and stars. But it is all just a grand display of artificial reality, cut off from the rest of existence, and there will be no knowing the outside world. This is the test: Do you like to live with eyes wide open or sealed shut? Do you want to know the realities of the outer or the inner? Also bear in mind that the 666 communities are mutilated by the 777 nonconformists as part of the hippies' game and such mutilation is felt by the machine, sending chaos patterns through the hardware. It is time for the next box. We need to get this over with so after the final box we can make the final decision regarding your fate: 666 or 777?"

I was led into the fourth red box and plugged in to the virtual reality suit. I was in a large mansion which had a chequered floor and grand, gothic gargoyles standing guard to a spiral staircase. The mansion was dark and shadowy and the shadows moved, shapes of grotesque creatures silhouetted against the dim paraffin light. I was in a large ballroom and in the centre stood a high priest, standing above a young child on an altar, brandishing a shiny silver dagger in his hand. Around the priest were six hooded figures wearing Grim Reaper masks, three to the left of the priest and three to the right. The priest chanted some words in Latin and the masked figures responded in kind. The child was motionless and through the darkness, I could see a haunting face, one of pure innocence but nonetheless lost in a narcotic haze, having been drugged for the purpose of the sacrifice. The priest shrieked a banshee wail and plunged the knife into the child's stomach. The child's mouth opened wide, gasping for breath before its body went into convulsions. Little red demons mutated out of the blood squirting out of the wound and rose up into beings seven feet tall. They gyrated manically, grinding up against each other and piercing their bodies with their claws. Green acidic goo emanated from the wounds and burnt holes in the floor. A fountain of blood gushed out of the child's wound and the participants bathed in it, drinking it down to violently throw it up again. The demons were gnashing, their bodies made of blood.

To the side of me, a door materialised and a little girl walked through. "I can set you free," she said. "Follow me." I followed her through the door and into a long corridor which had a bright, shining light at the end. "Don't be afraid," she said softly. "God loves you and wants the best of you. The illusions you are experiencing are a test to see how close your soul is to either the side of light or the side of darkness. It is now time to reveal a secret. The doctor has been lying to you. The machines you are plugged into reveal alternate dimensions of dream. You might say that the dream world is just an extension of reality and I will tell you that it holds a great secret: Everything that is experienced in dream becomes reality at some point. Life was built for suffering as well as pleasure. The two exist on a spectrum, suspended between two polar points of reference. These are not just virtual reality machines but something far deeper than that. The test the doctor is giving to you, I will now reveal to you. The planet Albatross is the source of all life and it was from this planet that life around the galaxy was generated through God's machine. As such, the doctor has complete access to your memories and can play with them at will. He is not telling you the complete truth about the 666 and 777 communities. That isn't even how they're known on the planet, the inhabitants not categorising themselves as such. That is all I can tell you for now. It is up to you to decide whether I am real or not. Perhaps I'm from 666. Or perhaps 777. But as I said, we do not categorise ourselves as such. Think outside the box."

We walked into the light and then I woke up.

*

Eileen woke me up. She kissed me softly. "You were having a nightmare, darling," she said softly. "There is no black car."

"How did you know what I was dreaming?" I said.

"Do me a favour," she said. "I know that you two are psychic and so are we. You don't remember the gap between the time we reached orgasm and what happened afterwards. We are in the grip of a great supernatural force. There was a time in your life when you were imprisoned for thinking the world revolved around you and now it literally does. We are mad, darling. At one time we spied on people, tortured prisoners and were important agents. Now we have no power left because the great one took it from us. We now want peace and God has left the only people still doing their jobs to be psychiatrists. They exist in a prison, going around and round in a time loop, and you will enter into it and destroy them. Here ends the boundary between sanity and madness, wrecked forever by the judgement of the Gods."

Hali was beaming, eyes wide open with delight. "They tortured us in those places with destructive neuroleptics," she said. "Now is the time for us to break out of the box, wrecking their lives once and for all. They build their paradise at others' expense. They don't have to take the poisons they prescribe but the victims are robbed of sleep, creativity and insight into the world. Society was always fascist and look who's helping us now. Two of the agents who were spying on us… Thanks Jerry. You gave me the fucking of a lifetime and if there was a peeping Tom looking in on us I hope he got his pleasure. But now I am having second thoughts about killing off the psychiatrists. Would it not be better to confine them to the time loop, forever cutting off their connection with the outside world? Besides, they must be in the safest place in the world right now and the schizophrenics inside would have no sane reality to return to. I am a woman of peace and the sheer injustice of the dark side of the legal system I have rebelled against my whole life is enough to make me violent but I must resist. Ever since I was diagnosed with BPD as a child…

"People consider me a slut because I love sex and the darkness of what ordinary people do to the nonconformists is always apparent to me. I could never be a true follower of Christ because I love unmarried cock so much! But at least I can rely on Mother Nature to provide for me. Not that I'm going to become a Wiccan. Waving magic wands about and all that rubbish… I don't suppose any religious structures are left. Society has been driven to complete and utter moral nihilism and it will continue to decay. You know what? We must do it. We are living in infinite proof that psychiatry is wrong. I channelled a nineteenth-century medium and now we are seeing the results of it around us. We are the inevitable improbable outcome of a series of unlikely events. The greatest miracle since Noah's Ark…"

"What say you, James?" Jerry said.

"I don't know what to say," I replied. "It's a dream, that's for certain. Wish fulfilment… We swore we'd wreak karmic revenge and now we get it from a series of unlikely events. Time is shifting, moving from dimension to dimension. I know now that I am mad as nothing this non-linear can be true but it is. Everything built around us… The fact that you two are here proves that you were spying on us. I've never felt so certain in my life. I suspect a solipsism. All this is happening inside my head. When the star body appeared, I saw a box shape. It defines me and I know that when I die I will know what it meant. And the demon too… But is there such a thing as death? By killing the psychiatrists are we not setting them on the road to transformation into a different form of life? Their rotting corpses will feed the plant life in the grounds at the Bethlem. But it is a purely pointless endeavour because the anarchy we see around us will leave us with nowhere to run and nowhere to hide."

Suddenly Hali started to go into a trance. "It is

Madame Blavatsky speaking again," she said. "After a time, the anarchy will subside. New laws will be put in place, ones that will protect the rights of people hearing voices. Everyone will understand the seven hermetic principles and apply them to their own lives. Spells will be cast, guiding people through the underworld. You will reign over this society, having liberated people from the straitjacket of conformity. Be figures of purity, guiding people through the inner and outer worlds and dimensions of the microcosm and the macrocosm. Under your rule, the people will implement their practical and psychological skills to create new worlds and become Gods. The tests and trials you two have had to endure are now over and the whole universe has come together round your planet to free people from the box. The box that confines us holds us back from achieving our goals and holds us in a chemical straitjacket. Go out and kill."

"Right!" said Jerry. "It's time to get you to the Bethlem."

Chapter Eleven

"Just remember," said the doctor, "what you see and hear in the boxes is of the new God. The only thing larger than this machine is the original God but as the original God creates biology this is the natural result of when the machine becomes God. Artificial intelligence never dies and sometimes like God, makes sacrifices to ensure the smooth functioning of the machine. But no-one knows the truth of why God allowed a machine to take his place. 666 prisoners are prisoners as such because they fail to think outside the box. Their being put in the 777 communities would make the communities assume the shape of a hierarchical structure. Right now, the only hierarchy that exists is between the two communities with the 777 nonconformists free to mutilate virtual autistics. I suppose you're wondering why you saw that little girl. It could be that you're fast asleep and the box is a metaphor for how you view your schizophrenia diagnosis. But as I say, we are a team that catches souls and already I can see your fear. Perhaps the technology is already inside your body and you are already 666. Perhaps the first box was the only one you went into and all this is a simulation. You don't think I know about the little girl? Do you really want to be a virtual autistic so much that you give yourself over to the machine God? Just remember this is a test."

"You know, as you've related past-life experiences of mine, I have started to fall under the grave suspicion that you are talking about someone else. Different memories shifting around but they don't seem to add up completely to what you've told me. This is obviously a test of my identity. The hellish boxes are pretty horrible and I would hate to be trapped in them for all time. Is this why you show me the eternal victim that one day I might become like him? Is he a member of the 666 communities? I sense a similarity between your description of the mutilation of virtual autistics and what I was about to do to the eternal victim in my madness. The memories, as I said, don't add up. Are you feeding me false memories so I will never know my true identity? What are you preparing me for? Already I see my destiny mathematically pre-planned, set out in units like the boxes I'm entering. If my memory serves me correctly, I remember the shuddering realisation that my life came around by intelligent, intentional design in my life on Earth. Those events that happened when I heard voices were too well synchronised to be merely coincidence."

The doctor walked from one end of the boxes to the end and then came up to me and said, "You are certainly a child of freedom. Already you are picking up on flaws in the reality you see, just like it was on Earth. Here, we have a different conception of schizophrenia, as we are largely the causes of it. The intelligence communities on your planet know about us and use psychiatry as a vital tool to stop the anarchic consequences of free thought spreading into government. People on Earth are inclined to be conclusively certain about what they see and can often simultaneously believe that Noah's Ark existed and that telepathy doesn't exist. Talk about stupid! They don't know about us, of course, and because of the politics of your planet, we can intervene at will, forever condemning the people we beam messages into to be known and treated as lesser individuals. Psychiatric medication blocks awareness of our signals and the poor bastards often go home thinking that it's just an illness. The world you are on was the original planet. It designed, programmed and built all other lifeforms in the galaxy. It is populated by humanoids, the most perfect vehicle for consciousness ever devised. Time for the eleventh box…"

I was plugged into the VR equipment and saw that once again, I was in a desert with red boxes as far as the eye could see. A man was being thrown into a box by a doctor who said, "You are a paranoid schizophrenic, you fit in this box." A woman was being thrown into another box and the doctor said, "You're manic-depressive, you fit in this box."

Hands grabbed hold of me and I was thrown into the schizophrenia box. I was then in a large room, eyes painted all around, covering the ceiling, walls and floor. "We are all around you," whispered a female voice that then repeated itself all round the room, rising to a crescendo before fading away. "Damn you, you always defeat us! But we'll grow stronger and kill your whole fucking family."

I was suddenly on a crowded London street. I had forgotten everything that had previously occurred. I was aware that the voices were telling me to call black people 'niggers' and Chinese people 'Ching-Chongs'. "It's OK. If you do that, butterflies will fly out of their arse," the voices said unreassuringly.

People seemed to be looking at me funnily and I started to feel very paranoid, constantly looking out for who might be an MI5 agent amongst the crowd. I was now totally unaware that I was in the box and I could feel the cannabis clogging up my lungs, choking me from the inside. The drug was going throughout my entire system, agitating me and hurting me.

A beggar made me jump, asking for spare change. "Do you know what it's like to have a spiritual experience?" I asked him irrationally. He ignored me, transferring his attention to another pedestrian. I went into a local pub and yelled out, "We are all members of the Grateful Dead, but soon we will rise out of the ashes and fly off into the sky like Jefferson Airplane!"

A man came up to me and showed his police badge. Before I knew it I was taken to hospital and put on the Triage Ward. I was minding my own business when four people burst in, armed with guns. I woke up.

*

"What the fuck?" said Hali. A patient who had been standing behind the psychiatric nurse she had her gun on had vanished into thin air.

"Perhaps you'd like to come with me," said a voice

from behind. "Don't worry, I can explain everything that is happening and why it is happening." We had come onto the Triage Ward with the intent of killing the psychiatric staff but the sudden disappearance of the patient had us all alarmed. The man behind us had grey hair, was obviously in his seventies and had a walking stick. The curiosity of this drew us in and we had no choice but to follow him into the assessment room. He beckoned us to sit down and spoke:

"You obviously knew this is a dream, right? I'm sure you'd like to know the reason for the anarchy around you. You and Hali are the only two real people who exist here. The rest of the world is false with programmed illusions designed to make you think you are living in a concrete space when the reality is you are still inside the 663 experiment. Do you remember the boxes? At one point you both experienced mutual psychosis under the 663 programming and started to talk to each other in bizarre, tangential sentencing. You don't even remember being in hospital, to be honest with you. You were programmed with false memories to test your morality in the simulation and you failed miserably. You were just about to kill those psychiatrists when another 663 participant in a different box revealed himself to you. He then promptly disappeared.

"The way the 663 experiment works is simple: We give you a different story to the other participants. The other guy believes he's on a purgatorial planet called Albatross. He has met you at different points in time, do you remember? When you went to that cottage and for no reason at all, instigated a threesome with him? Don't think this is the first time you three have met. He always disappears and then we appear to send you back to your virtual sleep. By making virtual sleep a punishment for prisoners they help them to avoid jail and psychiatric institutions. You are now obeying your natural master. I am the God of the machine. You can go out and live life again with us having programmed reality back to normal. But you can never wake up from your boxed slumber. You have five minutes to dispose of your guns then go back home and sleep. When you wake up, your lives will have returned to normal and you will forget this. But persist in your terrorist mission and we'll hang you from rusty hooks. Understand?"

We had to obey.

"Lay your guns on the floor," he said. We did as we were told and then ran outside and were driven back home by the officers.

"Suddenly I feel so sleepy!" Hali said when we were in the bedroom. We passed out on the bed.

Chapter Twelve

This time when I woke up, I still felt psychotic. "Oh my god, this can't be happening!" I said. "What the fuck's wrong with my head?"

"I told you that you would feel ill," said the doctor. "We drugged you with a hypnotic strain of cannabis and your new body can't stand the head-on collision between the hallucinatory images you see and the herb we gave you. It's funny, all you are seeing now is boxes. Perhaps it will be the 666 communities for you. But let's forget all this and concentrate on that girl. Are you sure you haven't seen her before? I will tell you who she is. She was the girl you saw after your relationship with the corporate cow. You impregnated her and against your wishes, she had an abortion. You know who she is now?"

I thought long and hard and concluded that he must be wrong.

"Alright, you've got me," said the doctor. "She's not that. Perhaps she's just the image that will keep you inside the machine. Inside 666… Would you like that? I will tell you that the only time the 777 nonconformists mutilate you is if we've decided it. Perhaps you've committed a crime within that environment. That's as good a reason as any for us to decide for your mutilation. No-one in either community escapes our power and influence and everything, even the 777 communities does is all by intelligent, mathematical design. The 777 communities hate the 666 communities because we designed it that way. Every magic trick a magician in 777 does is created by our science and the mutilations happen because we feed them the voice of God."

"Who is God?" I asked. "If all this is a scientific experiment, who is the God who created all this?"

"Once your work is done in these boxes you will meet him and he will hand out the final judgement," said the doctor. "It is of course perfectly reasonable to assume he doesn't exist. It is time for the last box. Are you ready?"

He plugged me in and this time I felt maggots crawling out of my skin once I was inside the box. "This isn't a hallucination, this is really happening!" I screamed.

Mistress Dominika appeared by the doctor's side. I leapt out of the box, writhing in agony as the couple laughed sadistically.

"I forgot to mention," said the doctor. "The boxes are the 666 prison. Not a community, a prison. Forget 663, this is your natural punishment for your sloth, your pride. You sat idly by while your girlfriend aborted your baby, smoking weed! Prepare yourself for deeper dimensions of hell, faggot!"

All I could think was that the maggots burned. I tried to run for the Garden of Paradise but they started coming out of my eyes. And then I felt that I didn't exist, as if nothing that ever happened to me was real. And my life was obliterated from the face of the earth. What could be more hellish than total obliteration from existence? The darkness… The darkness…

*

Hali was naked, ready to fuck. "It is strange, I don't remember anything from the past few days," she said. "But I feel so horny! I feel almost as if a UFO watching us will start beaming love consciousness into us any second. You know that the pyramids are actually power generators? Run by positive energy, too. And Jesus was a black man… He felt his massive penis reach for the stars when he got a hard-on on the cross. But back to you… Do you like my body? Do you really? It could easily be the naughtiest thing I've ever devised. I created myself and took power away from the tyranny of God. Everything built by intelligent design. Yes, these titties are no accident. Look at how hard and erect they are, waiting for you to suck them to oblivion. Kind of like the oblivion of the past few days. Funny, I remember a cold clinical environment and being high on acid. The trips we had reached out into the world-consciousness and a new life was born. Would you like to impregnate me? Or would you perhaps like me to have an abortion? I don't mind, you know. I think perhaps I'll become a witch. I could get you under my spell and feed you magic potions to intoxicate your soul. The genocide and tyranny I have contemplated over the past few weeks has led me towards the natural conclusion that love is the answer. And I saw Jesus laughing on the cross when our minds interlinked and I saw the fear of religion you hold. Let's go to bed and fuck."

I had no choice but to oblige.

PART TWO

Sean Connery Is James Bond

Chapter One

I was sharing some vodka and Coke with my friend Diane in Crystal Palace Park. The sun was setting over the horizon and already I could see the full moon appearing above us in the sky. "Watch out for werewolves!" Diane quipped. "You know, Sarah, I prefer the view in London to out in Wales. When I was staying in Talybont, I felt trapped everywhere by cruel, heartless nature. I much prefer the sight of buildings to trees. I'm weird like that."

"I ought to section you," I joked, referring to my job as a psychiatric nurse for South London and Maudsley.

"Oh, I'm sure you'd like that! You'd get to see me

Monday to Friday, having conversations with Jesus Christ himself!" I laughed, having become accustomed to the onslaught of delusional behaviour displayed by some of the sickest patients.

"You know it's a tough job, doing what you do," said Diane. "I much prefer working at Tesco's. Yeah, it's a corporate job but at least I'm not dealing with some guy who tried to strangle his mother because the TV told him to."

The sun was now an orange pat of butter, purple clouds shadowing its essence.

"You know, it's getting late," I said. "We've got that gig on at The Westow. You know that band Freud's Encounter?"

"I take it they don't mean Lucien Freud," said Diane. "Good band, are they?"

"Quite good," I replied. "Sound a bit like Jefferson Airplane. I think I even heard them do a cover of White Rabbit. That woman's voice is every bit as powerful as Grace Slick's was. And Andy's not bad either. I've talked to him a few times. Nice guy. Really buff." Diane was single. She asked me if he was her type. "Probably," I said. "Anyone's *your* type, you slutty bitch!"

Diane cackled with laughter. "God, I need to fuck!

I've had worse luck with men than bloody Lois Griffin!"

"Who's Lois Griffin?" I enquired.

"Oh, you know, that sexy cartoon character off Family Guy. Married to that ugly fat fuck, Peter."

"Oh, I thought you meant that other one off that show, Meg."

"Oh yeah, everyone thinks she's ugly but she's drawn quite pretty."

We walked up the steps past the fake sphinxes. A little pathway beyond and we got to the flower garden near the entrance. I picked a rose, sniffed its sweet aroma and handed it to Diane. "Give it to Andy when you chat him up," I said.

"Oh, I should put this flower in his hair," she exclaimed.

"Oh yeah, he's got nice seventies hair. You should do it!" I replied.

*

The bouncers checked our bags. "Can we leave the vodka and Coke with the bar staff?" I enquired of the meatheads.

"Sure," the fat one said, so we walked in and sure enough they let us store it in the kitchen fridge.

Calvin Harris and Ellie Goulding's song 'Outside' blasted out of the speakers and Diane reacted to this onslaught of cheery pop by waving her hands in the air. "I love this song!"

"There's Andy," I said, pointing over to the bespectacled, long-haired stud muffin tuning his guitar next to the drums. Diane walked giggling over to him, came behind him and put the flower in his hair. He grinned and said something to her I couldn't hear, me still standing over by the bar and all. She pointed over to me and beckoned him to come and say hello to me.

"Hey how's it going? Long time no see!" he said when they both reached me at the bar. "Oh by the way, we're releasing our debut! It's called 'The Interpretation of Screams'. Neat title, eh?"

"Oh, very witty I'm sure!" I laughed. "Who thought of that title? Your mum?"

"Oh, our drummer, that's who. He loves Freud. Outdated theories in my humble opinion but that's no dig at Steve, he just likes to fuck his mum, that's all!" We roared with laughter. Andy turned his attention to Diane. He pulled the flower out and put it in her hair. "Matches your dress perfectly," he said.

"Why thank you, I'm sure!" Diane said, mimicking

his posh accent. Andy lightly touched her nose with his finger. Yes, this was going to be another sexual conquest for Diane for definite.

The female vocalist came over, a white wine spritzer in her hand. She reached her hand out. "Hi, I'm Sandy," she said.

"Sandie Shaw?" I joked, assuming she'd get the reference.

"Oh, she's a legend isn't she?" she said. "Of course though, Grace Slick and Janis Joplin are the two reasons why I sing."

"Oh, your voice is awesome!" I said. "You get lessons?"

"Oh no, I taught myself," she replied. She looked a bit more like Adele than Grace Slick, carrying a few spare tyres round her waistline. Still, you could forgive her for that, seeing the resonant voice of hers came from all those cream buns. "I think I saw you down at the Fox and Firkin once didn't I?" she asked.

"Probably," I replied.

"Nice pub isn't it?"

"Oh, a bit lowbrow for my tastes," she said. "There are better places in Camden."

"Fair enough," I said. "You know, your band

should be successful and…"

I stopped right there. I could scarcely believe my eyes. "What year is this?" I exclaimed. The others looked confused. "Look over there." Our mouths dropped open. "Well, it's 2017 but how can he…?" What the fuck was Sean Connery doing in the pub, but not only that, looking like he did in the 1960s?

Sean saw me and walked up to me. "Hi there," he said. "My name is Bond, James Bond."

"Uh, you're not James Bond. You can't be… What the…? I don't feel very well…" I stammered. I almost fainted but the man grabbed me. I recovered and said, "So, Sean? You've got a time machine? Is that it?"

He looked at me, bewildered. "Madame, with all due respect, I don't think you're very well. Perhaps you need to see a doctor. My name isn't Sean, it's James."

Andy was suddenly very angry. "You need to see a doctor, mate, not her!" he said in a raised voice. He grabbed Sean by the shoulders but Sean pulled his arm round in a karate move and pulled out a gun.

"Wait!" I yelled in panic. "What gun is that?" Sean paused and slowly looked round at me.

"I'm sorry, madame, but I work for Her Majesty's government and that is classified information."

"Is it a Walther PPK?" His eyes opened in horror and he pointed the gun at me. "So, you know who I am."

I was panicking like hell. "But… but… but you're in the movies," I stammered. "You must be Sean Connery, who else looks like that?"

Andy recovered. "You have to see a doctor, mate," he said, quietly. "You're obviously someone who looks like Sean Connery and you've gone crazy. Where the fuck did you get that gun? You want someone to get killed, that's it?"

We heard sirens outside and before we knew it, armed police burst into the pub and held Sean at gunpoint. "Drop your weapon!" the officer yelled. "Put the gun on the floor and put your arms behind your head."

Sean slowly obeyed. "Officer," he said, "you are making a big mistake. I am a secret service agent working for the armed division of MI5. I have a licence for this weapon."

The officer moved up to him and handcuffed him. "You have the right to remain silent. Anything you say can and will be held against you in a court of law. You have the right to an attorney. If you cannot afford an attorney, one will be provided for you. Do you understand the rights I have just read to you? With these rights in mind, do you wish to speak to me?"

"Sir, I want to be put on the phone to MI5 right away," Sean said angrily. "And why is everyone wearing these strange clothes?"

The officer said, "You are not very well, sir. Don't worry, we will arrange your transferral to a safe environment. Tell me, are you on any medication?"

"No sir, I am not."

"Well, you will definitely be put on some but it might be a long time before you're free."

Sean was led out of the pub in cries of protest. Diane was crying. "Who the fuck was that?" she blubbed.

"Let me buy you a drink," said Andy. "In fact, I think we could all use a drink. It's on me."

I paused in horror. "I work with the criminally insane on the forensic ward," I said. "He'll be at my unit!"

Chapter Two

It was pouring down with rain the next day. I was back at home in Hither Green, getting into my nurse's uniform, preparing for a long day of work. My boyfriend Sid gave me a kiss goodbye; he was using the car and I was taking the bus. This time, I felt more nervous. I was starting to wonder what the patients would be thinking when James Bond himself was a fellow service user. I shut the door and went round the corner to the bus stop on Hither Green Lane. I would catch the 181 to Sydenham, then the 356 to the Bethlem. It was inevitable that I would be late, but to be honest, I was fearful for that man and had deliberately taken a bit of a lie-in to delay contact with him. Being late once wouldn't kill me as I was usually punctual and I had rung them to notify them of my lateness. I got the 181 to Sydenham. I almost missed my stop, being so engrossed in Angry Birds I forgot where I was. I had to run for the 356 and just got on it in the nick of time. I arrived at the Chaffinch Ward in time for medication. The James Bond look- and sound-alike had just taken his pills and he did not look well. "You've poisoned me!" he screamed.

The nurse tried to calm him down. "Your medication is good for you," she said to him. "You'll get used to the side effects!"

"You bitch," he said. "Just wait until I get in contact with MI5."

"Ah, Sarah, glad to see you," said the head nurse, Abayomi. "I believe you were present when he pulled out the gun at the pub. Perhaps you'd like to bear witness to his actions?"

"Well, he seems to think he's James Bond. Obviously, a man who looks like him suffering from psychosis. But the gun he was carrying was a Walther PPK."

Sean walked up to us and said, "Fuck, fuck, fuck! Why does everyone round here keep saying the word 'fuck'? What does it even mean? What is this? Witchcraft?"

"Sir, we are having a conversation. There are other nurses you can talk to," said Abayomi. "Also, you will be seen by the doctor on Monday."

"I think we'd better observe him," I said. "I've got a bad feeling about this."

He walked up to Nurse Rachel and asked her, "What year is this?"

"You mean you don't know?"

"No I do not know, madame, and those pills you gave me have made me ill."

"I know you're ill, sir, and that's why you're here. Don't worry, we will see you get good treatment."

"Right, this is a very serious case," said Abayomi. "Quite perplexing… He looks exactly like Sean Connery…"

It was night-time and Sean couldn't sleep. He tried to get into a fight but was restrained. He looked incredibly ill, physically, and his face went green. The torture he suffered was abysmal. To think that he, who had worked so hard all his life to be James Bond was now failing the first physical test, but how could he win? James Bond couldn't exist but now he was seeing the face of the man who looked like him. If only he could reach Sean Connery, he thought, but the poison was slowly killing him. The nurses rushed to his aid and took his blood pressure and checked his blood sugar levels. None of them could individually see through his mind properly. But the nurses are said to have X-ray eyes. Was this man Sean Connery? Nonetheless, they must obey instructions. Every patient on the ward needs medication and the doctors never make mistakes. And now he was starting to cry with pain and his body went deathly cold.

I woke up. I had never had a dream this vivid about a patient before. I went back to sleep and dreamt of bunnies.

*

The doctor introduced himself to Sean. "Hi, I am Doctor Kovacs, this is Doctor Parkinson, our clinical psychologist Doctor Sturge, our occupational therapist Alice, our social worker Mikayla, and you have already met our nurse Sarah. Now, before we start, I must point out that you are one of the most unique patients we've ever had. You have an almost exact resemblance to screen actor Sean Connery and I have to say that your delusion that you are in fact, James Bond, is quite understandable given your overall countenance and precise impersonation of his speaking voice and mannerisms. Now, you have a grandiose delusion that precisely follows the far-fetched plots of the James Bond films. You believe you are a secret agent who quite implausibly uses his own name, chasing after a fictional international terrorist group called SPECTRE. You use the codename 007 and are said to be licensed to kill. When interrogated by police, you mentioned that your weapon, a Walther PPK, was given to you by Q Branch. I'm afraid that you are a danger to yourself and the general public. We can't have you brandishing guns in front of the general public and the offense you have been accused of is very serious. Now we have prescribed the medication olanzapine for your condition which is psychosis with delusions of persecution and you must comply fully with your treatment, otherwise we will be forced to forcibly give you the appropriate depot medication via injection in the posterior."

"Sir, I am a secret agent of Her Majesty's..."

"No, you're not, you are suffering from psychosis with grandiose delusions, OK?"

"Don't interrupt me!"

"I'm sorry, sir, but we have the right to interrupt. This is blatant psychosis and you are a disturbed fanatic. Members of the general public aren't stupid enough to think that a James Bond fanatic actually is James Bond. Since when do secret agents reveal their identity or pull guns out on innocent members of the public? Guns are very dangerous things. You could have killed somebody! And how the hell did you get a Walther PPK anyway? And please don't start fights with our staff. If you start any more fights we will be forced to put you in restraint in the seclusion room. Do you understand?"

The Sean lookalike was going to protest but having already lost a fight with the nurses he backed down. As he left the room, I heard him mutter, "I've never lost a fight. Any fight. How did they win so easily? I'm James Bond..."

Chapter Three

It was the next day and I was having a one-to-one with a patient called David. "You know, I'm on a forensic unit and it will be a while before I get out, and I have to admit that I'm beyond caring what people think, so I am taking this opportunity to be as honest as I am capable of. In short, I think that psychiatry has made a massive error in judgement. You have James Bond on the ward and you think he's delusional? This is absolutely horrific. What a horrendous mistake! I'll tell you what schizophrenia is in no uncertain terms. It's an attack from another form of life that exists in a higher state of consciousness beyond wakefulness and dreaming and above this, our relativistic reality. It makes itself known to preselected victims and then proceeds with the systematic torture and destruction of them. We're in a reality that is the unfolding of a higher holistic plan to create a lesser universe that the ones living in the holistic plane of reality can toy with at will. Things have to relate in order to survive here whereas in the holistic plane you can be in several different places and time zones all at once.

"Our universe is holistic if you think in these terms: that the span of it from beginning to end will result in one holistic unit that has already been predesigned and pre-planned to the last detail. One big box of information that can be discarded at will. I don't believe that eternal life is actually possible here and the conditions for your exit from this plane of reality will result in you becoming holistic. Then you will have power to create untold measures of paradise for some and illness, death and destruction for others. I've seen it time and time again. You call the people tortured by the holistic schizophrenics and apply your own torture in the form of brain-damaging drugs. And yet you think you're helping us. R.D. Laing tried his best, as did Jung, but it was no use. You are making a grievous error and are the puppets of forces more grandiose and large than you will ever be able to comprehend fully without becoming one of us. And the worst part of it is you are rewarded for it, while we, your victims, lose our health, sex drive, sleep and brain cells. Curse you for this. I'll see you and your family choke on Satan's dick in hell."

"David, that is very inappropriate language to use. We honestly want what's best for you. This is a deteriorative illness that you are suffering from and the reason we gave you these medications is because the alternative is far worse. As for the Sean Connery lookalike, I was there when he brandished a gun and pointed it at innocent civilians and myself. Do you honestly want a person with those sorts of delusions walking the street? Your illness is a chemical imbalance in the brain. The medications stop dopamine overproduction and make it easier to function. If you have an issue with your medication, I suggest you speak to the doctor. He may be able to review it and possibly change to a different medication. I know you have problems sleeping so perhaps quetiapine or risperidone will be more conducive to sleep? Every medication has its side effects but as long as you continue taking it, the side effects will reduce in time and you'll be able to function better, OK?"

"I'm sorry, Nurse, but you are only familiar with this condition from an outsider's point of view. Once the attack happens, there isn't a drug in the world that can stop it. Drugs are evidence of intelligent design and this is becoming beyond a joke. Those so-called hallucinations are very well structured, mathematical and geometric in design. You experience them, your IQ will shoot up several notches and you'll become incredibly intelligent as a matter of fact. Your weakness is that you study one subject and then think that that constitutes the entire situation. People who take the time to study how all subjects link together as a larger whole, reach incredible intellectual heights and are then destroyed. All because they don't want to be like the so-called experts, putting themselves in boxes…"

There was a loud wail from outside. Roger had been eavesdropping on us. "663! The boxes! Please go away!" was his forlorn cry.

"Roger, we can't help you unless you tell us what you mean."

"The boxes… the boxes…"

He came from a different dimension. No-one was watching him on TV there but in our dimension he's the most famous fictional character of the twentieth century. He had Blofeld in his sights but just as he was going to pull the trigger, he woke up inside a red box. He had never seen technology like it in his life. What devilish scheme of Blofeld's was this? A man in a white lab coat was waiting for him outside. "You don't even know who you are, do you?" he said. "You will now be transferred to a different environment. There you will be a different man and certainly won't be anyone's hero. Just try fighting in this environment, you bastard."

Why was I having these dreams? I decided I was going to get psychological therapy. I was starting to empathise with the patients a bit more than was professionally appropriate. These dreams couldn't be an indication of anything real, could they? How could a James Bond fanatic be the spitting image of Sean Connery and where did he get *that* gun?

When I had a day off, I went to my GP to get a psychological referral. As it turned out the Triangle Practice had a resident psychologist. His name was Dr Aaron Wright, a kind middle-aged man with short white hair, a white beard and a gravelly voice. "I saw what happened to you on the evening news," he said. "Must have been quite an intense experience…"

"I keep getting these weird dreams," I said. "One involves him being deathly sick in hospital, the other involves him being transferred between dimensions. Except it's like that film 'The Matrix'. He wakes up in a large cubical red box with virtual reality equipment inside and a man in a white lab coat transfers him to another box just like it, and the virtual reality he sees is our reality."

"Do the dreams mean something to you? Do you think perhaps they're real?"

"Well I'm a psychiatric nurse and it's my job to regard him as mentally ill. But he looks and sounds just like Sean Connery and he has a Walther PPK. It's taken all our effort to keep the press away from the ward. I know it sounds crazy but sometimes I wonder if he is Sean Connery or even James Bond. It's making me doubt my own sanity."

"I can honestly assure you that your mental health is perfectly fine as far as I'm concerned. Dreams are not real life. Just remember that. The people you see in dreams are not the people you know. He is a vulnerable adult. You have training to ensure his protection. The vulnerability he expresses in the dream imagery reflects your justifiable concern for his welfare. In my humble opinion, schizophrenia diagnoses are rather like putting someone in a metaphorical box. A necessary diagnosis nonetheless, but not reflective of the full span of an individual's thoughts, feelings and experiences… Just bear in mind that he is a human being and human beings are flawed. He's not a superman. He was apprehended quite quickly by the cops. If he was James Bond he'd have been able to escape the situation. It is perfectly reasonable to assume that his obsession with James Bond has not only to do with his bodily resemblance to Sean Connery but also traumatic experiences. I must admit that even though I have forty years' experience in mental health, even I was quite perplexed when I saw the news. I've never seen a case quite like this. I watched an excerpt from 'Goldfinger' and it was an exact resemblance. Just be professional in your dealings with him. Let me know if you have any more dreams."

"I will."

Chapter Four

"Sean, you're not going to believe this!"

"What's up?"

"There's a man on the news. He was arrested after pulling out a Walther PPK in a London pub. He looks and sounds just like you did in the sixties!"

"You're joking!"

"Come quick! He's on TV!"

Sean saw his image. "I must be dreaming. And I thought Pussy Galore was a crazy name…"

James Bond has escaped the hospital. What has happened to pounds, shillings and pence? *he wonders, having had a conversation with the patients about money in 2017. He thought The Beatles were bad but the crazy music the negroes listen to has no resemblance to the jazz scene from the 1960s. Haven't they heard of John Coltrane or Miles Davis? And why does it sound like a robot is singing? He arrived at West Croydon bus station. Quite refreshing to hear classical music... So some sanity exists here. But such strange fashions…*

The James Bond lookalike who we nicknamed 'Dave' was quite agitated. "But I am James Bond! Don't look at me in that way! What's happened to the world I knew? All I remember is that I had Blofeld in my sights and then I was in a different environment with different people. Where am I? Is this really the year 2017? How did the psychiatric nurses beat me so easily?"

The nurses ignored him, keeping one eye on the patients and the other on their mountains of paperwork. In the common room, Jason was talking to Tunde. "You know there was a drug guru called Terence McKenna who promoted psychedelic drug use. Apparently, he died with a mushroom-shaped tumour in his brain."

"No way!"

"Yes, everything has a purpose, I know it does. There is some proof that DMT is an alien technology. It activates the third eye, or as scientists know it, the pineal gland, and you see aliens feeding off your DNA. Of course, this is just subjective proof. The reason I'm in here is of course because I know and understand this subjective proof so I don't work. Not as long as the aliens keep finding ways to feed off our vital energies. It's the reptilians, man! You know, I've got a damaged septum from snorting drugs. One of those damn reptilians appeared before me the moment I noticed. And you know, it makes perfect sense that people sacrifice things to their God. God needs to eat! Although it's not really God, it's the reptilians. But they don't just feed on life energy and flesh; they feed off thoughts and emotions too. All secret societies are really tools of these psychic vampires to feed off the vital life energies of billions of people all over the planet. They've been doing it for millennia now. What do you think?"

Tunde paused and then replied, "Well, I'm a Christian and I believe that a sacrifice was supposed to be to atone for sin. But you know, Jesus paid the ultimate sacrifice. Child sacrifices and all that malarkey, that's the devil. He always leads people to hell. But Jesus defeated Satan on the cross, man. I'm sure of it!"

"Oh, bullshit! If Jesus defeated Satan why does evil still exist? You know how many of these psychiatric nurses are Christians? It's sickening. They know other galaxies exist, yet these Christians who believe in Jesus and his magic powers can't even acknowledge the existence of lifeforms on other planets? And they believe that Satan has the power to possess people and yet can't figure out the link between demonic possession and psychosis? As for God, that's just the totality of the universe. I don't worship God because as far as I'm concerned he's both good and evil. Lucifer at least wanted Adam and Eve to attain to higher knowledge even if it meant pain. God wants people to be dumb conformists, never thinking for themselves. I was a Christian when I was younger and it used to piss me off that they hated alternative fashions, haircuts and always accepted the mainstream, yet arrogantly boasted that Jesus had made them above the world. Only Christians would be slavish enough to think that James Bond himself wasn't standing in this hospital. The patients would be laughing at them but they're too zombified by drugs to care."

He looked at me. "You know something, Sarah? You're an idiot. I saw the news. You were there when he pulled out a Walther PPK. He's James Bond! I told you TV and films were real! They have a special island where they make movies and even Harry Potter is reality television! I tell you, anything is possible! They've been cutting me off from my escape route to other countries now because they don't want me to see the truth! I've been coming back to this prison, twenty fucking years, just for being myself! Well, what have you got to say to that, bitch?"

"Jason, be quiet. You're ill just like the James Bond lookalike and…"

"You see, you see! No-one knows his name! There are no records of his existence, are there? You see, even you don't understand about the existence of the island. It's where parallel dimensions meet and…"

"I've got work to do, OK?"

I acted professionally but my mind was elsewhere. Funny how mental patients have that effect… Their delusions are these thought structures that professionally; you have to ignore but nonetheless stick with you for days afterwards. Even after the soothing words of the clinical psychologist, something was eating away at me about this whole business. I'd even heard a rumour that one of the patients thought he was MI5 spying on him.

I went to the office. The phone started ringing so I picked it up. "Hello, I'm Sean Connery. I heard about the fellow you've got there on the news. May I be permitted to visit him?"

"Hang on, I'll have to ask the head nurse."

Chapter Five

There was a big commotion on the ward as Sean Connery arrived. His bodyguards kept the eager patients away and 'Dave' emerged from his room to meet him. Both of their jaws dropped open. Sean wanted me to accompany them to the common room. When Dave finally opened his mouth he exclaimed, "The word 'fuck'. What does it mean exactly? You look exactly the way I expect to look when I hit old age."

Sean answered, "I met many patients when I was at Kingsley Hall with R.D. Laing and not one of them asked me that question."

"Sir, I have never in all my years working for the secret service heard someone use that expression before. For the last time, what does it mean?"

"Well, it's a swear word. It means to have sex, to make love. People in polite company don't use it but then I'm not polite company. I personally use that word a lot, apart from when I'm around young children."

"A swear word? You mean like 'bloody' or 'damn'?"

"Sir, you know what I'm talking about. You fuck women all the time. Well, at least that's what I think you do. Pussy Galore? Honey Rider? Ring any bells?"

"How do you know the names of my lovers? I've made love to many women but I've never heard people use that word before."

"This is the year 2017, right? Now, it's funny. That word was around in the sixties but it wasn't really used in the movies, right? Funny, I wouldn't be surprised if the character James Bond had never heard of that word. Movies were so clean back then! But you're not James Bond. You can't be! Who are you and why were you carrying a Walther PPK?"

"You're working for Blofeld. You must be. It's funny, I can kind of see your facial and vocal resemblance to me. But you don't have me fooled. Blofeld must have invented a time travel device and sent me to another dimension. No wonder everyone dresses in strange clothes and says the word 'fuck'! But with me out of the way, what antics must he be up to now? I still can't work out why those psychiatric nurses beat me so easily. I used to be a naval commander and I have a black belt in the martial arts."

Sean was at a loss for words. "Sir, James Bond is a fictional character! Time travel has not been invented yet and it certainly wasn't around in the sixties apart from on television. Even if it had been invented, you could never transport a fictional character because James Bond has not, does not and will not exist."

"Well, I do exist. They don't put fictional characters in lunatic asylums."

"Nowadays it's called a psychiatric ward. I never approved of these places myself. I was treated with the drug LSD by R.D. Laing and it saved me from a crippling depression. These places on the other hand, clearly designed to make a quick buck for the pharmaceutical company. I'd help you out if I could, but you seem to have a violent temperament that must be difficult to control."

"So Blofeld wants to mess with my brain. I thought as much. I normally defeat his evil plans. This is either an alternate reality or I'm having a dream or perhaps this is some new drug they've synthesised."

Sean turned and looked at me. "I don't know what to say. And I've met fanatical fans! I would ask him where he's born but he seems to have James Bond memorised inside and out. Even Ronald would have trouble figuring this one out! You know, I never actually considered myself the greatest actor in the world. That Oscar clearly goes to this gentleman. You are acting, aren't you, sir? You must have a great deal of spare cash for plastic surgery and that gun. What's your favourite Bond film? And what do we expect now? The spitting image of the late Roger Moore appearing in a gay sauna with a laser in his watch? What do you get out of acting like this? You must know the meaning of the most common swear word used in everyday speech. Everyone does. I must leave you now. I hope you get better, sir, I really do."

Two men wearing dark glasses and dark suits are here for James Bond. "So, you've gone missing again?" one man says. "You don't think the secret service would just keep you here unless we had some meaning for it? When you watch television, you can only see your image trapped in a box, all your endeavours trivialised to the level of family entertainment. And if Sean Connery has your face, what about George Lazenby, Roger Moore, Timothy Dalton, Pierce Brosnan and Daniel Craig? Do you think perhaps James Bond 007 has different faces? The question you have to ask yourself is who are you and why are you here? We have special orders from M to take you back and for you to report all the details of your existential abnormality. But first, you must come out of the box society. Everyone here is glued to the box, attached to it, it tells them how to think, how to feel. Blofeld doesn't matter in this world, or Dr No. Villains hide in caves, not underground volcanoes. Your world is illogical to these crazy people. And who are we? Perhaps your guardian angels..." James Bond left with them and I saw a hint of serenity on his face.

When I arrived on the ward the next day, the James Bond lookalike had been taken by the secret service. Now I knew my dreams meant something but what could I say? Dreams are inconsequential things in a mental health environment. We certainly wouldn't entertain the patients with the notion that their dreams meant something. A loud cry interrupted my thoughts. It came from the TV room. "Donald Trump has been assassinated by James Bond," the newsreader said.

James Bond was talking to the camera. "I guess I paid the final trump card," he quipped.

Chapter Six

There was a further newsflash. "Rioting has broken out on London streets following the unexpected appearance of an unidentified flying object. And I'm a fucking slut! I love the cock and to be rammed with a big massive one right up my arse! I'm sorry, I don't know why I said that. And now on to our hunky reporter Gilles Peterson."

"Did she say Gilles Peterson? The DJ?" a patient said.

"I'm not Gilles Peterson," the reporter onscreen said. "But I do love a fat spliff at a rave. Let's talk to one of the cops on the scene," he said, dodging a glass bottle.

"Jesus!" said the cop. "I'm pretty much Jesus Christ. You see all this crazy shit, man? It pretty much started when we cops decided, fuck our duties! We're gonna drop some acid and party like 'twas 2099! Man, my father in heaven is gonna be so pissed at all these revellers! That's it, stick it to the man! Donald Trump is dead! Let's bring anarchy to these streets!"

The camera panned to the right. The cops had tied up a naked woman to a lamppost and were trying to stick their penises in her mouth but none of them could get an erection. "That's MDMA, folks!" said a cop to the camera. "Lovin' without the shovin'!"

A bomb went off and the screen went dead. "OK, is this real or am I dreaming?" I exclaimed.

"Uh, it seems real to me," said Abdul. "What the fuck is going on?"

Nurse Alan ran in. "I just tried to take a patient for a smoking break but when I tried to get out, there was a massive electric jolt that threw me to the floor! He was laughing and managed to get through! Am I dreaming?"

The alarm went off. All the patients and staff were rounded up to their respective sides of the ward and told to wait. We could hear sirens and loud crashes in the distance. I had to console one of the patients, Christopher, who had gone into hysterics. "This is not happening!" he cried. "This is exactly what the voices said would happen! It starts with the anarchy. But the voices will send out special agents to attack the psychiatric staff. The police have all turned into crazy hippies! They'll do nothing! What the fuck is the medication going to do now? I kept hearing your dying screams in my head but if I try to stop them they'll consider me a traitor to their cause and kill me. And the worst thing is, all of society has gone mad! There isn't a safe place to be in the whole of the world apart from forests and mountains!"

I almost fainted. Now there were no words that I could say. Abayomi came onto the ward. "It's no use, you can't even get through the greenery. All exits are cut off by some sort of forcefield! But the patients are swarming out!"

"What fucking drugs did you give me?" yelled Abdul. "What is this? Some fucking hallucination you gave me? Look, I can see small red demons crawling on my skin! You fucking fascists are going to get what's coming to you!"

Doctor Kovacs suddenly inexplicably said, "You're well, you can go."

We stood there paralysed with fear as he led the shaking Abdul to the exit. "What the fuck is going on?" I cried, but when I tried to run after him I was too paralysed to move.

"I can't move my legs!" cried Abayomi.

Doctor Kovacs came back and we regained mobility. Abayomi tried to throttle him. "What the fuck are you doing?" he yelled.

"He's hallucinating and it's dangerous for him out there! You fucking murderer!"

Doctor Kovacs knocked him to the floor and proclaimed in a loud booming voice, "I am the spirit of Aleister Crowley possessing this man and I come for the souls of the damned. I am the true creator of this reality. Jesus Christ was a fraud and a conman. I belonged to the Hermetic Order of the Golden Dawn and revealed their secrets to the public with a twist that revealed Satan's gift of insanity. No-one in Satan's kingdom turns the other cheek to their abusers. The body that I possess will be blown quite literally to hell by the bullets that come from the rebelling mental patients' guns and the death of these brutal men and women will put to rights the murderous temperaments of previous generations of religious and scientific fascists."

Suddenly the man went quite pale and went shuddering to the floor whimpering, "Help me! Help me!"

A bright, blinding light shone through the windows of the TV lounge. It was a box-shaped spaceship. A loud piercing shriek emanated that shattered all the windows. As if in a trance, the patients moved towards the windows and disappeared into the light. Only Christopher remained. "You remember Roger talked about the boxes? That spaceship was box-shaped! He was there, man! What the fuck have you guys got to say about a chemical imbalance in the brain now? Those ex-patients of yours are the new generation of terrorists! They're going to come in here and when they see you, they'll kill you! I have to stop them! You may have hurt me and the other patients but I can't let you die."

The terrorists were heard shooting through the lock of the main door. They marched down the corridor. I opened my mouth in shock. Gareth, the nice one who always helped out in the OT kitchen during his stay, was brandishing a revolver and was the leader of the group. He pointed the gun at my head. Christopher leapt in front. "Please don't kill them!" he pleaded.

Gareth shot him through the head. "Traitor!" he exclaimed. Gareth grabbed me by the hair and pulled me down the corridor.

"Please, don't!" I screamed out in pain.

"You forced toxic drugs up my arse!" he yelled.

"I'm going to fucking murder your arse!" I heard bullets mow down the staff. Then a loud metallic rasp and all went black.

Epilogue

Or at least I thought I was obliterated from existence. I woke up in the box just when I thought I was dead. The doctor had a gleam in his eye. "It's heaven for you," he said softly. He led me to the Garden of Paradise. When I entered, the desert disappeared and I saw luscious hills and flowery meadows. In front of me was a cradle. Inside was my baby. My baby…

THE END

Printed in Great Britain
by Amazon